THE BEAT

Victims

Out they went, a hundred people examining every bin and skip, combing the fields around the embankment, looking under every piece of rubble in disused factories and warehouses, fingertip-searching wasteground near the football stadiums and any other place which occurred to the officers coordinating it.

The phone rang and Dylan answered it. He grunted a few times, made a couple of notes, then said, "We'll be there in five." He turned to Neil.

"Somebody's reported a body floating in the river."

Other titles in **The Beat** *series:*

Missing Person

Black and Blue

Smokescreen

Asking For It

Dead White Male

Losers

Sudden Death

Night Shift

Coming soon in Point Crime:

Lawless and Tilley: Fire and Water
Malcolm Rose

Playing Dead
Jill Bennett

The Joslin de Lay Mysteries 3: Hell's Kitchen
Dennis Hamley

Visit David Belbin's homepage at
http://www.geocities.com/SoHo/Lofts/5155

POINT CRiME

THE BEAT

Victims

David Belbin

SCHOLASTIC

Scholastic Children's Books
Commonwealth House, 1–19 New Oxford Street,
London WC1A 1NU, UK
a division of Scholastic Ltd
London ~ New York ~ Toronto ~ Sydney ~ Auckland

First published in the UK by Scholastic Ltd, 1998

Copyright © David Belbin, 1998

ISBN 0 590 11357 7

Typeset by TW Typesetting, Midsomer Norton, Somerset

Printed by Cox & Wyman Ltd, Reading, Berks.

10 9 8 7 6 5 4 3 2 1

The city in these pages is real. The events described in them are not. All of the characters, together with the police station where some of them work, are imaginary. The author wishes to thank the many people, including serving police officers, who helped him with this series. He alone is responsible for any mistakes.

1

These days, it was hard for Ruth Clarke to get out of bed in the morning. Especially now that October was about to turn into cold, grey November – *and* all the people she shared a house with had already deserted the sinking ship which was her life.

Sam, Ruth's landlady, had cleared off on a cheap package to Tunisia with Steve, her on/off boyfriend. Gary, who Ruth worked with, had more or less moved in with his boyfriend, Umberto, now that the footballer's mother had returned to Italy. And Clare Coppola, Ruth's best friend, was off work, injured. Clare had moved in with *her* mother, who was helping her cope with a bereavement. None of the above had deserted Ruth deliberately.

Nevertheless, she felt obscurely betrayed by the lot of them.

Five-thirty. Ruth sloped out of bed and dressed quickly. No time for a shower. If she hurried, she'd be able to stuff down a mug of tea and some toast before driving to work, where she would have to see the one person who had *really* betrayed her: PC Ben Shipman. Ben had been her boyfriend for five months before leaving her for a street trash seventeen-year-old. Ruth still woke nights and sobbed her socks off over it. But at work she became the ice queen. John Farraday, her new partner, thought that Ruth was a hard bitch. If only.

She managed one slice of toast and half a mug of tea and would have been at work with two minutes to spare if the car had started first time, which it didn't. It would have to go. No one drove 2CVs any more and certainly not police officers, but this relic had been all she could afford when her Volkswagen gave up the ghost. Maybe she should take out a loan before the winter really set in. On earlies, you needed a reliable car.

Jan Hunt was giving the briefing. It was the usual stuff: car thefts, crack dealers, burglaries, bail absconders and missing teenagers. The sarge was looking her age, Ruth thought. She wouldn't see thirty again. Beside her, Gary looked chipper, as ever. Next to him, Ben Shipman avoided Ruth's gaze, the way he always did these days. He was still heart-breakingly handsome. It was his birthday tomorrow. He would be twenty-four. Ruth would not be sending him a card.

The sarge paused.

"A word of warning," she said. "Alan Wallace, forty-four, formerly of West Bridgford. Ring any bells?"

"Likes little boys," John Farraday commented.

"And girls," Jan said. "He's not fussy. A convicted paedophile. He did five years for various offences. Moved into the area six months ago. Within a month, Bridgford were on to him for indecently assaulting two kids he'd babysat and a nine-year-old boy who lived next door but one. His case comes up today."

"Don't tell me," Tim Cooper said in his cynical voice. "You want us to provide him with a police escort, ensure his safety?"

"I wish that was all," Jan said. "But we've been informed that the Crown Prosecution Service aren't going to offer any evidence. He'll be free by midday."

"*What?*" Ruth said, outraged. "How can that be?"

"No witnesses," Jan told her. "The neighbours he babysat for have moved and don't want their children to have anything to do with the case. The nine-year-old was supposed to testify, but he's been in counselling for six months and now that push has come to shove, the parents don't want him in court. A conviction's not guaranteed and the parents think the trial would make his trauma worse."

"He could give video evidence, surely?" Ruth suggested.

"That's what would have happened, but you know how it works: the child's put in a room with an adult he's never met before and asked to talk about an intimate betrayal with a camera pointing at him. Some kids cope with that better than others. The parents have decided against. So Wallace is being let out. The prison has been informed, and they've told Social Services and Probation. I gather he's been found a hostel place on the edge of the Maynard Estate. Villiers House."

Gary's eyes widened. "You know where that is, do you, Sarge?"

"I just said—"

"Because I know exactly where it is," Gary went on, his jaw tightening. "It's right opposite a nursery school."

Charlene Harris showered, then dressed, beginning with the pink silk slip which her bloke had bought her the week before. They'd been going together for nearly two months now. He was always buying her gifts: nothing too flashy, just nice things to show that he appreciated her. Normally, wearing silk against her skin made Charlene feel good. This morning, though, nothing would stop her from feeling dirty.

Ian had nearly finished his breakfast. He was twice her age and needed less sleep than she did. He put down his *Daily Telegraph* as she came in and told her there was tea in the pot.

"I want fresh coffee," she said. "Something to zap me into gear."

"Tough day ahead?"

"The Wallace trial."

"Ah," Ian murmured, considerately. "Those are never easy. Let me make that coffee for you."

"S'all right."

She didn't like the way he made coffee. It was never quite hot enough or strong enough. Charlene put four spoonfuls of beans into the black coffee grinder she'd bought him for his forty-eighth birthday and turned it on. When the noise finished, Ian was speaking.

"...wanted to specialize in crime. You have to get used to cases like—"

"I know, I know," Charlene interrupted him. "But people like him make me feel..."

She stopped herself, not wanting to sound unprofessional. Ian Jagger wasn't just her boyfriend, he was also her boss.

"You're worried he'll get off, aren't you?" Ian said.

"The barrister thinks he'll make mincemeat of

the little boy. There's no way for the defence to bring in his previous or the attack on the kids he was babysitting. So, yes, I think we'll get him off. But he did it."

Ian nodded sagely. "They're all guilty. If not of what they're charged with, of something else, often something worse. But they're all entitled to the best defence we can give them, no matter what their crime."

"And when he does it again?" Charlene asked, pouring the coffee into a filter paper, using a finger to shake free the brown deposits which were stuck beneath the grinder blades. "How do I stop myself feeling guilty then?"

"You'll learn to live with it," Ian said. "It goes with the job."

A couple of minutes later, he was on his way to work. Ian liked to arrive before everybody else. It prevented gossip about his affair with Charlene and allowed him to get a head start on all of his employees. While her coffee brewed, Charlene sipped orange juice and forcefed herself the muesli which Ian had thoughtfully got in for her. It was not her usual brand. There was too much fruit.

Her boyfriend was a clever man. (*Boyfriend* seemed liked the wrong word for a man his age, but what else was there? *Lover* made it sound like Ian was married. In fact, he was a widower. *Partner* was nearest, but too formal, reminding her of work.) Ian never offered easy solutions. The world was always grey, never black and white. He was easy to like, harder to trust. Sometimes, still, Charlene suspected his kindness. His morality was so complex. Maybe it amounted to no morality at all.

Still, Ian Jagger did good when he could, which was more than you could say for most people. It would be easy to fall completely in love with him, but Charlene hadn't given that much of herself, not yet. The age difference was too big, for a start. They wouldn't last. But she would learn as much from him as she could before they agreed to part.

Charlene set the burglar alarm and followed him to work.

Curt was late for school, but stopped off for a can anyway. A bell rang as he entered the shop. The newsagent had a new owner, Mr Simons, but he wasn't there. No one was.

"Just a minute," called a voice from the back.

Curt waited, surrounded by sweets, cigarettes, newspapers and magazines, all there for the taking. He knew this shop. There was no hidden video camera. The new owner was a bit green, or he wouldn't leave the place unattended, not round here. Curt was wearing a coat with big pockets: a shoplifter's special. All he had to do was reach out and…

The door opened again and Curt breathed a sigh

of relief. Saved by the bell. The boy who entered was from his school, his year, too, but Curt had never spoken to him. Until now.

"You doing a paper round here?" the youth asked. He was returning one of those yellow paper round bags, empty, and would be late for school himself.

Curt shook his head.

"Where's the old man?"

"In the back."

"Nice one."

The youth reached over the counter, grabbing two packets of twenty, then offered one of them to Curt.

"No thanks," he said, "I don't smoke."

The youth shrugged and shoved both packets into his pocket before Mr Simons came back through.

"You're late, Trevor," he said, before turning to Curt. "And what can I do for you, son?"

Curt bought his can and left in a hurry. Cigarettes were no longer the only thing that he'd given up. His girlfriend would be proud of him. His sister too. His mother, on the other hand, would have told him off for not taking the fags and giving them to her. But Mum's opinion didn't matter any more. This time, she'd taken off for good, leaving Curt to his sister and the social workers.

Rapid footsteps followed him.

"Curt, innit?" It was the paperboy from the shop.

"Yeah."

"Trev. So what did you get just now, before I come in?"

Curt hesitated. Telling the truth would make him look soft. But if Trevor spread it around that Curt was thieving again, it could mess up his new scene, and he was trying to keep his nose clean. Any day now, the social workers would try to take him into care. He didn't want to give them an excuse.

"None of your business," Curt told Trevor, putting on his hard man face.

"Ah, come on, what do you think I am? You didn't grass on me. I'm not going to tell anyone, am I?"

Curt tried to stare him down, but Trevor wasn't having it. He wanted to be mates. Curt, if truth be told, didn't have any friends, not unless you counted Natalie.

"Two Fuse bars," he told the boy.

"Nice one." Trev hesitated and looked around. There was nobody within earshot, so he went on. "You've been around a bit, haven't you? I heard you hung out with some pretty big-time burglars."

So big-time that both of them were inside doing time, Curt thought.

"So?" was all he said.

"So I've got a proposition for you. Easy pickings. Want to hear it?"

2

Charlene was flabbergasted.

"They're offering *no evidence*? Wallace has been inside for five months!"

"He's lucky not to be doing five years," the barrister said, quietly, then looked round. "I think the client wants a word."

Alan Wallace was grinning broadly as he approached. He had a kind face. There was a slight goofiness about his eyes, making him appear vulnerable, which led people to trust him. Until it was too late.

"You did brilliantly," he said.

"We didn't do anything," Charlene said. "The little boy refused to give evidence, even by video link. You got lucky."

"Let's go for a drink to celebrate."

"Sorry," the brief said. "I've got another case."

That was a blatant lie, because this case was due to run for at least a week, but it got him out of the court. Charlene, however, couldn't escape so easily. Ignoring the drinks offer, she began to spell out Wallace's options now that he was out.

"Have you got somewhere to live?" she finished.

"My stuff's in store. I can't really go back to my old place, can I?"

They were interrupted by a middle-aged woman in a polo neck sweater. "Excuse me, Mr Wallace. I'm the court liaison probation officer…"

The woman offered to get on to the council, find him temporary accommodation.

"Where will it be?"

"They've just reopened a hostel in the Meadows, Villiers House. There'll probably be a place there."

"What do you think?" Wallace asked Charlene. "Should I go?"

Wallace was a free man. He was under no obligation to go where he was told or to report his whereabouts.

"Have you got anywhere else?" Charlene asked.

"No. But you could—"

Charlene shook her head. "Not part of my job description, sorry." She turned to the probation officer. "Perhaps you could give me the postal address?" The woman wrote it down for her. "Can you find him a group?" Charlene asked, while

Wallace went to the loo. "Somewhere that might help…"

"If he'll go," the woman replied, "which I doubt, there's a modular course that he could join at any stage. It's meant for convicted offenders…"

"He's been convicted in the past."

"Like I said, if he'll go voluntarily, we should be able to get him a place." The woman went to make a phone call as Wallace returned.

"I want to discuss compensation," the paedophile said. The studied look of shame was starting to ease from his face. He was beginning to realize that he was free.

"Ring the office," Charlene told him, hurriedly. "Make an appointment." If she was lucky, she'd be able to get someone else to deal with it.

Half an hour later, Ruth and John were entering the last hour of their shift when they saw a dazed-looking middle-aged man getting out of a car.

"Is that him?" For the last hour, they'd made a point of doing frequent circuits around Villiers House in their patrol car, waiting for Wallace.

"Looks like it," John said. "The woman driving'll be the social worker or probation officer, one of those."

"Think we ought to go and introduce ourselves?" Ruth suggested.

"Wait till the woman's gone. Some of those cows

are on the wrong side – she might start telling us his rights."

Ruth thought that John was wrong, but said nothing. She'd moved from Nottingham South, where she'd had a sexist, prejudiced partner, to East, where she'd got more of the same. Still, it could be worse. Inspector Winter could have paired her with Ben.

Across the street from Villiers House, the children in the Happy Days nursery were singing nursery rhymes. Ruth shivered. Then she saw the social worker coming out.

"Let's have a word with her first," she suggested to John.

"Whatever you say. You're the boss."

At least John was easygoing. He hadn't wanted to check out the nonce – after all, Ben and Gary were covering this beat on foot – but when Ruth insisted, he went along with it.

"Excuse me," Ruth managed to catch the woman as she was closing the car door. "Can I have a word?"

"About what?"

"Alan Wallace."

"It's starting to rain. You'd better get in."

They introduced themselves. The probation officer's name was Ellen Thomas.

"He's cooperating," she told Ruth, "which he doesn't have to. He could vanish tomorrow if he had anywhere to go. There's nothing to stop him. But he's nice, for a pervert. Says he'll go on a course starting next week. Though maybe he only said that to get me off his back. He's a lucky man – still in shock about getting out. Prison's a tough place for men like him."

"We're very worried about him being opposite the nursery."

"Oh, don't be. I've checked the files. He's never offended against anybody younger than six. But someone ought to have a quiet word with someone at the local Primary School – make sure they know that Wallace is there. Get the Head to do an assembly about going with strangers, that kind of thing."

"We can't do that," Ruth said.

The police were only allowed to do what was called a "community notification" on the authority of an Assistant Chief Constable, and even then only after a "risk strategy" meeting with all the professionals concerned.

"Someone ought to."

"You may be right. My partner and I thought we'd go and see Wallace now, have a word, frighten him into keeping his nose clean."

"Big mistake, if you ask me," Ellen said. "He already knows that you're watching. You might frighten him into doing a runner. At least for now we know where he is."

Reluctantly, Ruth took her advice.

*   *   *

"Curt?" It was Mr Walker, Curt's Head of Year. "Your mother hasn't made an appointment to see me on parents' evening yet."

"Er … no, sir. She's working. She won't be able to come."

Curt kept walking but the teacher grabbed his shoulder. He hated it when teachers touched you like that.

"Wait up, Curt." The teacher lowered his tone and began to speak confidentially. "When we said we'd take you back, your mother agreed to keep in close touch with the school."

"I'm doing all right, aren't I?"

"Better than we expected," Mr Walker admitted. "But if she can't make parents' evening, I would like your mum to come in for a chat, so that we can check we're all working from the same map, so to speak."

"I'll get her to give you a bell," Curt said.

"Good lad." Walker let him go.

How long before the Head of Year found out that Mum was gone for good? Had the social worker been on to him? Curt wouldn't be surprised. Julie had done a pretty good snow job on one who came round the other day, pretending that Mum was still on a long holiday. But that story wouldn't hold up forever. Any day now, they'd be back to take Curt into care.

Curt knew what care was like: a cacky children's home where half the girls were on the game and some of the lads, too. It was the last place on earth he wanted to be. How long had he got? Curt would go on the run before he let them take him into care. He'd even team up with that toe-rag, Trevor.

Actually, the more he thought about it, the more Trevor's plan seemed like a pretty good one, almost foolproof. And next week was half term, perfect timing. But Curt wasn't having any of it. Barely two weeks ago, he'd gone in the river, could have drowned. He'd fractured two ribs in the crash. He'd been lucky not to fracture his skull, too, the doctors said. He'd been given a second chance, and he was going to take it.

When he got home, Julie told Curt that Social Services had phoned. They wanted to see Curt and Mum together, tomorrow. It was crunch time.

"I put them off, told them it wasn't convenient. They weren't best pleased, said they'd find you one way or another."

Curt swore, then told Julie what Walker had said at school.

"Perhaps if I went to see him at the parents' evening tonight," Julie thought aloud, "told them I'm looking after you while Mum's been delayed abroad…"

"I can just see that!" Curt said. "You talking to

the teachers about me. Most of them taught you, too. They know why you messed up all your exams."

She'd been pregnant with Tammy at the time.

"So what?" Julie said. "I'm not embarrassed. Are you embarrassed?"

"No, but … you're not even eighteen. If you go acting as my … guardian, they'll know something's up. They might get on to Social Services straight away."

"I don't think schools work that closely with Social Services," Julie said. "You know, we're going to have to do something."

Tammy began to cry and Julie put on a bottle for her. "It's Ben's birthday tomorrow," she told Curt. "He's on earlies and I want to pamper him a bit. Could you go to Natalie's straight after school, stay over maybe? Do you think her mum would mind?"

"I'll ring her," Curt said. He'd been going to anyway.

He left it ten minutes until Natalie was sure to be home from school, then dialled. She answered on the first ring.

"I'll ask my mum and ring you back," she said, after he'd asked. "I don't know if she's out or still in bed."

"All right." He hung up.

Curt wasn't much good at talking on the phone. He wondered about Maxine, Natalie's mum, still in bed at four in the afternoon. She'd taken it bad when Gordon, Natalie's dad, did a runner with all their money. They were totally skint. Maybe Maxine stayed in bed to save on the heating bills.

"Well?" Julie asked.

"She's calling me back."

"I was thinking," Julie said as she gave Tammy the bottle. "Do you want me to ask Ben if he could help sort out the Social Services? They might bend the rules for a copper."

"You're kidding!" Curt said. "What's he going to do, adopt me?"

"You could do worse," Julie muttered. "I can remember your real dad. If Social Services tracked that waster down and made him face his responsibilities, you'd be begging to be taken into care, believe me."

Curt said nothing. He and Julie had different fathers, the same mother, all three of them useless. He knew next to nothing about his father, which was fine by him. What you didn't know couldn't hurt you.

The phone rang. Natalie.

"Sorry," she said, "Mum's putting on a moody about you being here all the time. And school just sent a letter about me not doing homework." Curt swore. "But listen," Natalie went on. "Mum's new bloke's taking her to some posh hotel on Sat'day. They're staying over. I've told her I'll spend the night at a mate's, so I thought … if you wanted to come then."

"You're on," Curt said, then closed down the conversation. He didn't want Natalie knowing how bad his situation was. He wanted to sort it first. Trouble was, he could be in care by Saturday night.

3

Midday. The early shift was into its final hours and a light rain had begun to fall. Ruth decided to go back to the station and catch up on some paperwork. She OK'd it with Jan first. It was a known fact: there was less crime when it rained.

"Seen Clare lately?" the sarge asked.

Ruth shook her head. "I think she visited her dad at the weekend. I'm seeing her Friday night." Today was Wednesday. "Trouble is, neither of us are very good company at the moment."

Maybe Ruth would call in on the way home. They were best buddies. Ruth didn't need to be invited, did she?

"Penny for them."

Ruth looked up. It was Gary.

"Avoiding the rain?" Ruth asked him.

"Nah, the Inspector wants a word with Ben. Don't know what it's about. I was wondering, any chance of a lift home tonight?"

"I thought you didn't live with me any more," Ruth quipped, like a deserted lover.

"Umberto's off on International duty."

Gary's boyfriend was a first team footballer for Nottingham Forest and a regular in the Italy squad.

"Sure. I'll run you home later," Ruth said. "I could do with a chat, actually." She'd leave calling on Clare for another day.

"Yeah," Gary said. "We ought to catch up. I'll cook you dinner."

So Gary still cared. That was something.

Just before lunch, Curt saw a familiar figure walking past the classroom: his social worker. He felt like bolting then and there, half expecting her to turn up in the lesson and take him away. Nothing happened, except that he couldn't concentrate any more. He had trouble concentrating at the best of times. He needed to talk to Trev, who was in the room next to his. But Mr Carr, the Media Studies teacher, kept Curt behind, wanting to know why his mum hadn't been at parents' evening the night before.

It took Curt most of the lunch hour to find Trev. Despite the rain, he'd cleared off down the bank for a smoke. Curt explained the situation quickly.

"So you're into my plan, are you?"

"Maybe," Curt said. "Mainly, I need somewhere to live."

Trev smiled smugly. The tables had turned. Curt needed him.

"Meet me after school," he said. "There's a place called Villiers House."

Curt knew it.

"I stop there for a fag break on my round. About four, yeah?"

"Yeah."

Curt went to register for the last time. What would he do with his days when there was no school to go to? In summer that would be no problem, but the weather was turning dirty. He hated winter. Still, he'd be pretty busy if he followed the plans that Trevor had for the two of them. Sooner or later, though, he was bound to get caught. What the hell! Glen Parva couldn't be any worse than what he'd heard about local children's homes.

"Curt?" his form teacher called out.

"Yes, sir."

"Mr Walker wants a word with you. Get over there before your next lesson, would you?"

"Sir."

Curt picked up his bag and left. He wasn't going to see the Head of Year. The social worker was bound to be with him. They'd take him in. Curt knew that he could abscond from the children's home, but he wouldn't have time to meet Trev then. Anyway, it was a point of principle: having been arrested was one thing, being put in a home was another. It made him look bad.

Curt shot through the car park while registration was still going on. Fewer teachers around to ask him where he was going. Soon he was heading down the old railway cutting, back towards the Meadows. Curt was on his way to Villiers House. He'd find somewhere to hang out and wait for Trev to turn up.

Ben hadn't got the measure of the shift's new Inspector yet. He knew what this meeting would be about and it wasn't to wish him a happy birthday. A lot of coppers were tolerant of other officers' sexual shenanigans, taking the view that *There but for the grace of God go I*. A new breed were on the rise, however, who played everything by the rule book and were only concerned about covering themselves against criticism.

The new Inspector had removed the cacti which Inspector Grace used to keep on his filing cabinet, replacing them with a framed photo of his wife and kids. There were children's drawings on the wall, and his shelves were stacked in such a disorderly way that they were already overflowing. The Inspector pointed at a chair and Ben sat down.

"Is it true?" Winter asked, without defining what "it" was.

"Who told you?" Ben wanted to know what the Inspector knew before he fessed up to anything.

"That doesn't matter."

"Someone from this shift?"

"It doesn't matter," Winter repeated. "I want to hear it from you."

Ben deliberated. "I don't see why my friendship with Julie Wilder would jeopardize my job in any way," he said carefully.

"I'm glad you mentioned Ms Wilder yourself," Winter said. "I'd like you to explain the nature of your relationship with her."

"Why should I?" Ben protested. "Julie's clean. No criminal record. No suspicion of any criminal activity. Yes, we're quite close. Yes, I got to know her through the job – it's a matter of record that she's been a useful informant. What more do I need to say?"

"Are you living with her?"

"No."

If Ben was living with anyone of either sex, he was bound to inform the Inspector.

"But you don't deny that you have an ongoing relationship with her."

Ben didn't want to get into the whole nature of his relationship with Julie.

"This is humiliating, sir. Why don't you say what you've got to say and get this over with?"

Winter looked irritated. He didn't like people

telling him what to do. Especially not a black bobby barely out of his probation period.

"I shouldn't have to spell it out for you," he said. "We all like a bit of rough now and then. No problem, as long as you're discreet. But you're spending half your time with a slag who's on your beat—"

"She's not a—"

"All right, all right, but she's not a nun, either, is she? Had a kid when she was sixteen, so I'm told. The point is, she's on your beat. And her family is poison."

"Nobody's responsible for the rest of their family."

"A police officer is," Winter said. "If Curt Wilder were your brother, you wouldn't be allowed to work round here, would you?"

"No, but—"

"Listen, Ben. You know that Shirley Wilder's done a runner with Eddie Broom. Between you, me and the garden gate, DI Greasby informs me that there's a distinct possibility of Broom having been involved in my predecessor's murder. Now Julie is virtually Broom's daughter-in-law. In addition to which, her brother's about to be taken into care. He won't go quietly. And you're up to your neck in it. You don't want to be any more involved with the Wilders than you already are."

* * *

Villiers House had a big porch with bells for each of the flats. Curt checked and found that the door was on the latch. He didn't need a key to get into it. Perfect. He stood inside the porch, thinking, idly watching the walls of the nursery across the road. When he looked up at the sky, to see if the rain was likely to stop, he saw that someone else was watching, too. A middle-aged man sat in the bay window of a first-floor flat, staring into space.

Poor sod! Curt thought. I hope I don't end up like him, lonely and washed up in a stink-hole like this, watching kids whose life is only just beginning. Thinking about kids got Curt on to his niece, Tammy. He'd miss her and Julie if he had to hide out. How often would he be able to go back without getting caught?

"Excuse me."

Curt turned around. It was the man from upstairs. He had lines beneath his eyes and a decrepit cardigan, but his smile was kind, unthreatening.

"I saw you standing there. Are you waiting for someone?"

Be polite, Curt thought. Don't want this guy calling the caretaker, or, worse, the cops.

"That's right," Curt said. "I'm early."

"You look wet. I thought you might like to come up to my place, dry off. I can make you a cup of tea if you like."

Curt looked at his watch. There were over two

hours before Trev would show up. Why not?

"Thanks," he said, following the man up the dingy stairs. "Appreciate it."

Ben was silent. He knew that the Inspector wasn't exaggerating about the Wilders. He and Julie didn't discuss Eddie Broom, but anything was possible with a crook like him – up to and including murder. Even so, Ben couldn't let Julie go.

"I'll give you until next week to ease out of the affair gently," Winter said, standing up to indicate that the interview was over.

"A moment more, sir."

The Inspector looked irritated. "Yes?"

"What if I can't do it? Give her up, I mean."

"Then you'd better apply for a transfer, pronto."

"That wouldn't look good on my file," Ben complained. Besides which, he didn't want to move.

Winter gave him a sour look. "You should have thought about that before you started giving her one."

There was a knock on the door. Winter opened it.

"Sorry to interrupt, sir," Gary said, "but we've got a missing two–year-old on the Riverside Estate." He paused, obviously taking in that the two men were in the middle of some kind of row, then added, "I can take Ruth with me if you still need Ben…"

"No," the Inspector said. "We're done. Off you go."

Ben followed his partner out without saying another word. He hadn't agreed to anything, he reminded himself.

Curt wanted to get out. This guy – *Call me Alan*, he'd said – was too friendly for someone old enough to be his grandad. He'd made the tea then splashed some whiskey in it without asking whether Curt wanted any. Then he'd offered to let Curt choose a video to watch. And he kept asking questions.

"How old are you? Thirteen?"

"Fifteen." Curt knew he looked young for his age, but never thirteen.

"Got a girlfriend?"

"No." He wasn't talking about Natalie with some stranger.

"Boyfriend?"

"*No!*"

"Just asking. Would you like some more whiskey in that?"

"No, really. I'd better be going."

"What's the hurry? Your friend isn't here yet, is he?"

Curt didn't reply.

"You might like this video. *Electric Blue*. I picked it up cheap at the video shop last night. There are a few fuzzy bits, where people have paused it. Well, you can guess why."

"Not my scene, thanks."

Blue movies were for virgins and saddoes, as far as Curt was concerned, but *Call me Alan* took it the wrong way, moving next to him on the edge of the armchair.

"I bet you could use some money," he said.

"Who couldn't?" Curt replied. Maybe this was about to get interesting.

"You know," Alan said, "I've been away for a long time. I got very lonely…" When Curt felt the man's hand on his knee, he froze.

"You know what it's like to be lonely, don't you?"

The hand moved up Curt's thigh and he jumped out of the chair.

"Pervert!" Curt let loose a string of other swear words and the man started telling him to calm down.

"I thought you wanted it! I thought you wanted it! I'll pay. Listen, I've got money. How much do you—"

But Curt was already out of the room, charging down the stairs, through the porch, back into the pouring rain.

4

The Riverside Estate was an exclusive development on the city side of the River Trent, a short walk from the cricket and both football grounds. Most of these trendy, architect-designed places on the river were for singles or child-free couples, but Riverside was aimed at families. The apartments were low, streamlined buildings in reddy-brown brick, with big windows and double garages. Ben wouldn't mind living somewhere like that himself, maybe even with Julie, if he could afford it.

Funny, Ben had never hankered after living with a woman before, but Julie brought out the nesting instinct in him. He'd grown fond of Tammy. She ought to have a brother or sister to play with before the age gap grew too big. Not that he and Julie had discussed stuff like that. It was early days. If it weren't for the Inspector, putting pressure on him to finish with her, Ben probably wouldn't be thinking this way. He didn't like people telling him what to do in his private life.

Gary, his partner, thought Ben was mad, going out with a Wilder. But Gary was gay and therefore, Ben reckoned, couldn't tell how good-looking Julie was. Nor did he know how nurturing, smart and sincere she was. He knew nothing.

"I think it's this one," Gary said now.

"Right you are."

They found the address which had dialled three nines.

Gary didn't know that today was Ben's birthday, and Ben wanted to keep it that way. As expected, Ruth had said nothing in the parade room that morning. From now on, Ben wanted to keep his private and his professional work totally separate. It wasn't as if any of the other officers were friends of his outside the job (ex-girlfriends didn't count, he decided). He and Neil Foster were friends, but Neil was no longer in uniform.

"This is it."

Number 12A. Funny how some places still avoided using thirteen. You'd have thought that superstition was well on the way out, like years with a one on the front of them, but no. And the substitute number had turned out to be unlucky all the same.

The mother came to the door. As Gary talked, Ben sized her up.

Jenny Jackson was a thirty-something pro-fessional who'd taken time out from Telecom management to have a kid, just the one, and went back to work within a couple of months. She shared a nanny with a neighbour in a similar situation, but the nanny was sick today so Jenny had had to take the day off work. Now she was guilt-stricken and tearful.

"Bridget – that's the woman I share the nanny with – was meant to be leaving work early to take over so that I could at least show my face at the office this afternoon. I'd left the door on the latch so that she could walk in."

"As could anyone," Gary pointed out, gently.

"Yes, but I was doing the laundry – it's hard to find the time – and I might not have heard the bell. Anyway," she pleaded, "it's very safe round here."

Ben didn't comment. This development might attract people with a joint income well in excess of forty grand a year, but within five minutes (walking, not driving) you could find the highest percentage criminal population in the city, not to mention squats crawling with crackheads and hostels full of ageing itinerant dossers who would probably prefer prison to their current life and therefore had nothing to stop them committing any criminal act which took their fancy.

"When did you last see Tom?" Gary asked.

"Three-quarters of an hour ago. About one. He was playing in the living room, just round the corner from me. We were talking. He's picked up quite a few words. Then I took out one load, put in another. When I looked again, he was gone."

"Does he walk yet?" Ben asked.

"Yes. For a couple of months now. He can shift around quite quickly."

"Can he reach the doorknob?"

"Well, he tries. I've not seen him turn it yet, but obviously that was the first thing I thought. I've been round the neighbours, knocking on doors, finding out if anyone's seen him."

Wasted time, Ben knew, if the boy had been taken. She ought to have called the police straight away.

"All right," he said, taking over from Gary, who was only a probationer. "We'd better get a few more details. Do you have a recent photograph?"

When they were done, both men searched the apartment, which was standard procedure. Missing children sometimes turned out not to be missing, but hiding. They went from room to room, inspecting dust beneath beds, expensive clothes hung haphazardly in wardrobes, three TVs, two videos and a set of golf clubs. But no kid. Ben radioed Inspector Winter.

"You'd better start a door to door," Inspector Winter said. "I'll inform CID, send John and Ruth over to help. You're on overtime."

Great. Overtime on his birthday, and working with Ruth. That was all Ben needed.

Half the apartments had no one home. The next shift would come around later when the owners were back from work. Not that they'd have seen anything. Ben met an assortment of nannies, housewives and harassed home workers. The owners were all of an age (mid-thirties) and a type (pretentious professional). One claimed to be an accountant.

"Look, I'm awfully busy. No, I haven't seen anything. Recognize him? No. Sorry. If I see anything I'll call you, but I've got a client coming round, so…" The man, who was short and suffering from premature hair loss, began to close the door.

"I still need your name, sir, and the names of any people living at this address."

"Here's my card." It said his name was Jeremy Tate. "I live here alone."

Peculiar that, Ben thought, as he joined Gary. Why would a single man be living in a three- or four-bedroom apartment? He made a note.

When they returned to 12A, Jenny Jackson was starting to crack up. Her son had been missing for nearly two hours and the enormity of the event was beginning to sink in. At least she'd been joined by her husband, Tony, who was comforting her. He was a good deal older than Jenny – mid-forties, maybe. Second marriage, Ben guessed. Second family.

"No news, I'm afraid."

Tony Jackson ignored Ben and turned to a figure in an armchair. Ben hadn't noticed that there was anybody else there.

"What do you do next?" Tony Jackson asked.

Neil Foster nodded at Ben, then went through the procedure in detail. This was CID's case now. Everyone deferred to the man who wasn't wearing uniform.

In the months since he'd moved to CID, Neil had changed, Ben thought. He dressed better. His hair-cut was neater, more stylish. Maybe it was the job, or maybe it was the influence of his student girl-friend, Melanie.

"How's it going?" Neil asked as they were leaving the Jacksons.

"Can't complain."

"There's a story going round that you're having it off with the Wilder girl. What's her name? Julie."

"Who told you?" Ben asked, awkwardly.

"Jan mentioned it in passing," Neil said with a grin.

Neil remained friendly with Jan Hunt, who used to be his mentor. Was it her who told Winter? She wasn't a gossip, but might have regarded it as her responsibility.

"Not serious, is it?" Neil asked, catching Ben's uneasy mood.

"Serious enough."

"Happy birthday, anyway. Got plans?"

"Family stuff."

"Have a good one."

Actually, Ben was joining Julie as soon as he got off. They would spend the rest of the afternoon in bed, undisturbed, because Curt wasn't coming home. Also, she'd found a sitter for the evening so they could go out for a meal.

"Hey, Neil!" said a familiar voice. Ruth Clarke.

"Hi, how are you?" Neil said, as Ben beat a hasty retreat from his ex.

What was it with women and him? Ben wondered. One ex-girlfriend had followed him from London to Nottingham, where she worked as a criminal lawyer. Charlene's name had come up representing the pervert who got let out yesterday. He kept coming across her. Then his next ex went one better and actually moved on the same shift as him less than a month after he'd dumped her! Mad. Totally mad.

As Ben closed the door, Ruth gave him one of *those* looks – a mixture of pain and contempt. He could have done without that on his birthday.

Charlene had been unable to palm off the interview on anyone else, so at four on the afternoon after Alan Wallace had been freed, she met him to discuss his options.

"I lost nearly six months of my life," Wallace said.

"Yes, I know."

Charlene had prepared all the paperwork for the case. She'd advised Wallace that his "not guilty" plea had a good chance of success, while being privately convinced that he'd done exactly what was alleged, and a lot more.

"I had a job before I was arrested."

Not much of a job, actually, supervising pork pie packers in a factory. Before being convicted the first time, Wallace was deputy head at a primary school.

"So what can I do?"

"You don't have many options, I'm afraid," Charlene said. "You see, from a legal point of view, the courts were entitled to keep you in custody while waiting for trial. The prosecution convinced the magistrates that there was a real risk of your either reoffending or interfering with the witnesses, who were vulnerable children."

"But none of them was willing to testify against me!" Wallace complained.

"True," Charlene said, "and if they were adults, you'd be entitled to pursue a compensation claim against them in a civil court, arguing that they made the story up to get at you. But they're kids – even if you were allowed to sue them, they haven't got any money."

"There must be some way I can claim," Wallace protested. "Isn't there some kind of Criminal Compensation Board?"

"That's for victims," Charlene explained, patiently, "not offenders."

"I am a victim," Wallace said, straight-faced. Charlene clenched her fists beneath the desk. Sometimes the human race's capacity for hypocrisy could still surprise her.

"Look," she said, "your only avenue of redress would be to sue the police for malicious prosecution."

"Let's do that then."

"However, I have to advise you that your chances of success are zero. The police acted properly all the way down the line. If you took them to court, all you'd be doing would be drawing attention to yourself. Believe me, the media would have a field day."

"So you're saying that there's absolutely no way I can get any compensation?"

"That's right," Charlene said. "But look at it this way: you're free. You'll get benefit. It's a lot better than being in prison."

"Oh, thanks a lot," Wallace said, getting up. "My

life's ruined and I'm supposed to be grateful that things aren't worse? Thanks a million!"

You were grateful enough yesterday when they dropped the charges, Charlene thought, but didn't say. She watched him go out, grateful herself, and said a silent prayer that their paths would never cross again.

Ben was asleep when the doorbell rang. At first he thought that he was at home, but then it rang again and he remembered that he was in the Maynard Estate. He'd done an hour and a half's overtime before being relieved and heading straight over to Julie's. Now it was five to five. The bell rang again. Tammy started to cry and Julie swore.

"I was going to pretend not to be in. Better answer it now."

She opened the window, yelled "Hold on!" then tidied herself up and went to the door. When Ben went after her, he watched from the stairs. There were two officers from the shift that replaced his in the front room: Mike Singh and Stuart Crane. With them was a woman who could only be Curt's social worker. The woman was talking.

"I'm sorry, Julie, but I checked your story with the holiday firm whose name you gave me. They haven't got a Shirley Wilder on their client list."

"I must have got it wrong."

"She's been gone nearly a month, Julie. I don't

think she's coming back."

"So? Listen. If Mum don't come back, I can look after Curt. He's fifteen. I don't see what the problem is."

The social worker wasn't having that. "You can't control him. Did you know he skipped school this afternoon?"

"I—"

"Curt isn't your problem, he's ours. You have a baby of your own to look after. I'm sure if you explain the situation, the council won't throw you out of this house. Housing Benefit will pay the rent. But you can't afford to support Curt."

"I manage!"

Ben worried about what wasn't being said. Was Julie cheating the DHSS, like her mother used to? Was it illegal for her to claim Child Benefit for him, using her mother's book? She'd promised Ben that she didn't break the law, but her concept of legality was flexible.

"I'm sorry, Julie," the social worker went on, "but you're still only a kid yourself."

That wasn't the way to talk to Julie.

"Just shut your mouth!" Julie shouted, sounding like her mother. "What right have you got to come in here laying down the law? And why've you brought these bully boys with you, huh?"

It was a while since Ben had seen Julie's temper. He either had to make himself scarce or weigh in immediately. Happy birthday!

"We're here to help collect Curt," Mike Singh said, taking over. "Take him to the children's home. Where is he?"

"I don't know."

"You won't mind if we take a look…"

"Yes, I bloody do mind—"

"Hold on," Ben said, making himself known. The three invaders turned to face him. "Curt's not here. He's not coming back tonight, either."

"Where is he?" the social worker asked.

"I don't know," Ben said. "Look, can't we work this out?"

"He's in the job," Mike Singh told the social worker.

"We can talk," the woman said, "but it won't make any difference."

5

By Thursday lunchtime, the search for Tom Jackson was in full flood. That day's *Evening Post* had a photo of the boy on the front page. Every house within a one-mile radius of the boy's home was being canvassed. Each house or apartment on the Riverside Estate had been visited four times. All nearby areas of rough ground and disused buildings had been searched.

At the station, as her shift ended, Ruth was approached by DS Dylan.

"Excuse me, duck, have you got a moment? I need a little help."

He explained what he wanted. "Tracey's sick and I need a woman along."

Five minutes later, Ruth was on overtime. She'd changed into casual clothes at Dylan's request.

"What're the Jacksons like?" she asked, as they drove to the Riverside Estate.

"Pretty ordinary couple. Big age gap – that's the only odd thing. Nothing known on either of them, but we've done a bit of digging. Got some information this morning."

"And?"

"Tom Jackson's an only child, but he isn't his father's only child. He's the third. A daughter from Tony Jackson's first marriage – twelve now. And there was another son."

"Was?" Ruth asked.

"That's right. Died when he was fifteen months old. Suspicious circumstances. Cot death. The coroner said it was accidental, but…"

"Once might be an accident, twice looks like a pattern," Ruth said.

"Presuming the missing child's dead," Chris corrected her. "I want to do this gently. Get the Jacksons off their guard while they're relieved that we haven't recovered a body. I'll question the husband – he might not have told the wife about the first child. I want you to talk to her, ask for a cup of tea, follow her into the kitchen, something like that. Are you up for it?"

"Sure," Ruth said.

"Good girl." Dylan patted her on the knee. This

made Ruth uncomfortable, but she said nothing. It was a reflex gesture on Dylan's part, she thought. Nothing to complain about. Especially since, one day, she would like to be in CID.

Jenny Jackson let them in, a frail woman with a frightened face. She looked as though she were expecting to hear the worst at any moment. Dylan told her that there was no news.

"Tony'll be back from work any minute," she said. "Can I get you a drink?"

"I love your place," Ruth told Mrs Jackson, following her into the kitchen. The woman nodded distractedly. Ideal homes weren't much use when you'd lost your son.

"How long have you been married?" Ruth asked, when the kettle was on.

"Three years. Second time round for both of us. I thought I'd left it a bit late for a family, but Tom came along almost straight away. Recently, we've been trying for … for…"

Mrs Jackson began to cry. Ruth comforted her. She couldn't work out how she was going to ask this woman if she knew about the death of her husband's first son.

"Tell me what you're doing," Jenny said, brushing the tears from her face with her hand, which she then wiped by pushing back her hair.

"There's been another house-to-house," Ruth

said. "We've visited everywhere within a one-mile radius except for places which are empty or where we've confirmed that the owners are away for some reason."

"Have you got people looking in the river?" Jenny asked.

"No. There's no evidence to suggest that..."

If the police began dragging the Trent, it would be because they assumed that Tom was dead. But he'd only been missing for twenty-seven hours.

The front door slammed. Tony Jackson was home, looking harassed and haunted.

"Any news?"

Dylan repeated what Ruth had just said, adding details about the checks they were doing in the area.

"What about this child abuser they've just let go? Have you searched his place?"

"We've no grounds to do that, sir," Dylan said. "Nor have we any reason to suspect him. But we'll liaise with our Paedophile Investigation Unit, make sure we keep a very close eye on anyone with a record of..."

The tea was already made. Now Ruth had no excuse to get Jenny Jackson on her own. She stared out of the window, waiting for Dylan to make his move. A youth was coming down the path. He delivered the evening paper, then moved on. She thought about questioning him, but it was too late in the afternoon. By the time the boy had done his round the day before, Tom Jackson was long gone.

She took her tea and sipped it. Dylan gave her a beseeching glance. He'd got the father talking about the company he worked for. Ruth turned to Jenny.

"Could you show me Tom's room, please?"

"The other officers, yesterday…"

"It'll only take a minute."

It was a nice enough room. Square, with red racing cars on the wallpaper. Ruth praised it.

"Your bedroom's next door, is it?"

"Yes. Even so, the walls here are so well sound-proofed, we have to use a baby-minder intercom, or we can't hear if he cries in the night, not unless he really bawls…"

Ruth was trying to think how to turn the conversation round, but there wasn't a tactful way. She pretended to be examining beneath the bed.

"Does Mr Jackson have any children from his previous marriage?" she asked.

"One. A girl, Charlotte. She's just started secondary school."

"Just one," Ruth murmured, hoping the pause she left would draw out details of the other son, the one who died. But Jenny Jackson said nothing.

"The daughter, Charlotte," Ruth said after getting up. "Are you in close contact?"

"Oh, yes," Jenny said. "Frequent weekends, holidays … we get on well. She's due to come to us tomorrow, but I don't know whether it's a good idea or not. She's very fond of Tom, you see. When Tony rang to tell her, she was frantic, wanted to come at once. Do you think it's a good idea for her to stay with us?"

"I don't know," Ruth said. She wasn't very good on fathers and daughters. "If she wants to be here, then maybe it would be for the best…"

"Yes," Jenny said. "That's what I think. Tony isn't so sure."

They rejoined Chris Dylan and Tony Jackson in the living room.

"The sergeant thinks we ought to do a TV appeal tomorrow," Tony told Jenny.

"Whatever you say," Jenny said.

"If you could both take the morning off work," Dylan suggested.

"Of course," the father said.

"I'm on sick leave," Jenny told them. "I couldn't go back to work with this going on."

Dylan drove Ruth back to the station.

"Got time for a drink?" he asked. "I'd like to chew things over with you."

"Sure."

There was nothing to go home for. In the Forest Tavern, they were serving *tapas* these days. Chris paid for the drinks and Ruth ordered a plate of chorizo to stave off hunger.

"What do you reckon?" the sergeant asked.

"The mother didn't mention the boy, the one who died."

"Did you ask her directly?"

"No. How could I put it? *Did you know that your husband had another son who died mysteriously?* What did he say?"

"What you'd expect. It was a cot death, terrible shock. He hinted that it hastened the end of the marriage. Thanked me for not bringing it up in front of his wife."

"He said she knew about it?"

"Yes."

"I'm not sure if I believe that," Ruth said.

"Me neither."

"So … what next?"

"You tell me."

Ruth shrugged. "Talk to the first wife?"

"Smart girl," Dylan said.

"Another?" she asked.

"No, ta. I'm driving. And I'm babysitting my kids tonight."

He talked about them for a couple of minutes, every bit the proud father. Ruth hadn't realized that Dylan was divorced. He didn't wear a ring, but many didn't these days.

"I'll drop you off at home," he said.

"My car's at the station. I'd better go there. Technically, I'm still on overtime."

"I'll drop you off there then."

"Thanks. But don't bother. It's not far to walk."

"Rubbish. You're out of uniform. A girl's not safe on these streets."

He helped her on with her coat. *Is he interested?* Ruth wondered, as he took slightly too long about it. *Oh, stop kidding yourself. He's just being nice.* At least someone was.

"Maybe – if I OK it with your boss – you could help us out again tomorrow," Chris suggested, outside the station.

"Love to."

"All right. G'night."

Ruth went in, signed out and drove back to her empty house.

"Where's Curt?" Ben asked, when he joined Julie after work. He'd done some overtime, going house to house in the hunt for Tom Jackson, so it was gone four.

"Dunno," she said. "School rang up. He wasn't in today."

"You don't seem surprised."

"And I've had Social Services round again," she told him.

"No police this time?"

"No. Was that thanks to you?"

"I don't know."

Ben still hadn't told Julie about Inspector Winter's ultimatum. Things would be a lot easier, he thought,

if Curt *was* taken into care. Ben didn't mind Curt –
could even see his good side sometimes – but he'd
prefer him out of the way.

"Penny for them," Julie said.

"I was just wondering where Curt's going to stay
tonight."

Julie gave him a cuddle. "You really care, don't
you? You're a lovely man, Ben Shipman."

"Not as lovely as I seem," Ben said.

"Modest, too." She kissed him. "Come upstairs,
while Tammy's asleep."

"Don't mind if I do."

Later, he got up to go home. Ben needed unbroken
sleep before an early and Tammy still woke around
two.

"That *is* the reason, isn't it?" Julie asked when
he mentioned how the baby woke him. "You're not
getting grief at work for going out with me, are
you?"

"Nothing I can't handle," Ben assured her.

"You'd tell me if there was a problem, wouldn't
you?"

"Course I would."

"That's all right then."

She was sharp, he thought, as he took the last 90
bus across the city and along the Mansfield Road.
Julie knew more about human nature than either of
his exes. He found it hard to lie to her. Was he really

willing to take her on? It was too soon. But a decision had to be made.

6

"The Jackson parents are making a TV appeal today," Jan told the early shift, "so expect to be approached by members of the public, particularly if you're pulling overtime. Anyone else wanting to work until six, let me know by nine. Now, I want everybody out, and on foot."

"Ah, come on, Sarge!" Tim Cooper said. "It's raining."

"We need to be seen. CID are giving a briefing at eleven, so be back then if you can. Oh, and if anybody sees Curt Wilder – you all know what Curt looks like?"

Ruth glanced at Ben, who lowered his head. Everybody else nodded.

"...then pick him up. He's meant to be in care.

Social Services—"

"That isn't our job," Gary complained. "If Curt doesn't want to be put in a home, why should we—?"

"Little sod ought to be in prison, if you ask me," John Farraday said.

"Whatever," Jan told them, "we're to pick him up for his own protection. Orders. Now, get going."

Gary and Ben went out in a pair. Tim Cooper went on his own, but Jan stopped him. "John, go with Tim, would you? I'll keep Ruth for rapid response in the car."

Tim swore and John didn't look too happy either. The two men were usually paired together until Ruth joined the shift. Now they seemed to have fallen out.

"Seen Clare?" Jan asked. She was Clare's tutor officer.

"Not for a week. But I'm going round to hers for dinner tonight."

"Story is you were giving CID a hand yesterday."

"They needed a female and I was the only one around."

"Rather you than me," Jan said. "Cases like the Jackson one really get to me. That kid's practically the same age as Henry." Henry was her son.

"We'll find him," Ruth said, unreasonably confident.

Jan didn't respond.

＊　＊　＊

When a child under five has been missing for two days, Major Crimes are called in to work alongside the local beat officers and CID. Before Major Crimes was set up, coppers would be drafted in from other areas, leaving those shifts short for dealing with the day-to-day crime which never stopped.

It wasn't officially two days yet, and wouldn't be until midday today, Friday. But national press journalists, not content with letting the local stringers cover the story, were starting to arrive in the city. Pressure was coming down from the Chief Constable to get the case solved, and quickly. DI Greasby was putting pressure on Neil Foster, as the first *investigating* officer to arrive on the scene, to get a result. Neil was discussing it with Chris Dylan.

"Chances are," Dylan said, "that the kid's dead by now."

"Murdered?"

"Or gone for a swim in the Trent of his own accord. Either way, a goner."

"All right," Neil said. "So if he's been murdered, who did it?"

"Four times out of five, a family member. Do you fancy the father?"

Neil shook his head. "He was at work. Witnesses put him there all day."

"So what?" Dylan said. "The wife would be

covering for him. Maybe they did it together."

"Why?"

Dylan laughed. "Don't give yourself a headache, Neil. Remember this. There are five 'w's: *who, what, where, when* and then, and only then, *why*. Don't ask the last question until you know the answer to the other four, because otherwise, you'll be wasting your time."

"Fair enough," Neil said.

"Did you double-check that paedophile, Wallace – the one who got let out the other day?"

"I did," Neil said. "He'd only been in the area a day when the child went missing. He'd have had to move pretty sharpish to get to the Riverside, know in advance that the door was going to be open and have somewhere to hide the boy. In addition to which, he doesn't like kids under six, not according to our records."

"All right. Only we've had half a dozen calls from people who'd read about him being freed in the paper, day before the kid went. Citizens concerned that we'd made the connection."

"Amateur detectives," Neil commented.

Dylan shook his head. "Just people who'd rather make a fool of themselves than do nothing."

"I guess," Neil said, not used to Dylan showing a soft spot.

"You'll feel different when you've got kids yourself."

"What's the plan after the press conference?"

"I'm going after the ex-wife. See her at work. Might take Ruth Clarke with me again. Helps to have a woman on a sensitive interview like that."

"Jan Hunt's back," Neil pointed out. "She's got a kid the right age. Women respond to another mother."

"Good point," Dylan said. "I'll think about that. And do me a favour, triple-check Wallace personally. What's his alibi?"

Neil had called on Wallace the night before, listened to a long moan about him not getting compensation for the time he'd spent remanded in custody.

"He says he was in his room until two-thirty, then went to see his solicitor. I haven't checked with the solicitor yet."

"Do it. And find out if anybody saw him or phoned him in his flat."

"I'll try."

"Major Crimes are running down the other paedos in the area," Chris went on, "so liaise with them on that whole angle. You never know what the computer will come up with."

Notts Police had a computer database run by the Paedophile Investigation Unit. It listed not just convicted paedophiles, but people the police had serious concerns about – for instance, the owners of houses where missing kids showed up. You had to be suspicious of middle-aged men who invited youngsters round to watch videos or use the internet.

Then there were people who'd been cautioned or interviewed in respect of paedophile offences. The National Criminal Intelligence Service defined a paedophile as "an individual who has an unhealthy/ sexual interest in, or promotes a sexual interest in children". It included people who distributed child pornography or organized overseas "sex" tours. There were a lot of people on the database.

Dylan left and Neil rang Major Crimes. So far, they hadn't come up with any leads at all. He was glad that he wasn't working his way through the computer database himself. It was unpleasant work, and unlikely to be fruitful. He'd been on a course after he joined CID and knew that the majority of child abusers weren't anonymous strangers, but people the child already knew: family members, foster carers, stepfathers, babysitters – some kind of caregiver.

If Tom Jackson had been murdered, then the person responsible was most likely to be familiar with the family, which was the angle that CID were pursuing. But it was equally likely, in Neil's view, that Tom Jackson had wandered away and was trapped somewhere, maybe alive, maybe dead. Comprehensive searches had been made, but an even bigger one was about to be set up.

Kidnapping had been more or less ruled out. It was nearly two days now, and there'd been no ransom demand. But it could be that a very clever and ruthless kidnapper was waiting for the parents to get good and frightened before demanding a huge sum to return the child.

Someone could have kidnapped Tom, meaning to bring him up as their own – some messed-up woman who'd miscarried, maybe, or couldn't have kids. But people like that usually went for much younger babies. The police were very careful not to play up that scenario in situations like this because every time a baby was snatched from a hospital, there was a spate of copycat kidnappings. That was the last thing they wanted. But kidnap for adoption was still a possibility that the police had to keep in mind.

Neil checked his watch. His girlfriend had a late start on Fridays so she should still be home. He rang to say that he had a lot on, and probably wouldn't be able to pick her up from university after work, as promised.

Melanie didn't seem too bothered.

Curt woke at ten and didn't know where he was. Then it came to him: he'd got into this place with a plastic card and a screwdriver the night before. It wasn't much of a house. There was the usual: TV, video, a lousy old hi-fi. The retired couple who lived there had cancelled all their papers because, when the weather turned cold, they went to live in Malaga and stayed until spring set in. As long as he wasn't noticed, he could stay as long as he liked.

Trev had kept his part of the bargain, finding Curt a safe place to hide. But it had taken him a long time to get to sleep last night, hence the lie-in. He dressed, went downstairs and made himself a brew. He'd bought food and turned the fridge back on. The front room had net curtains. Therefore, as long as he kept the sound down and didn't put a light on, he was all right watching TV during the day.

The house was an end terrace, so there were neighbours on one side only. Chances were that next door had been given a key and asked to keep an eye on the place, redirect important mail, that kind of thing. So Curt left little trace of himself downstairs. If he heard someone turning the lock, he could be hidden in ten seconds, less. There was a cupboard under the stairs and he kept its door permanently open.

Trev would be round after school with details of their first job. He'd come to the back door. Until then, Curt was stuck with Richard and Judy and whatever films showed up in the afternoon. As he sat watching with his morning brew, two uniformed coppers walked by outside. Instinctively, Curt ducked. The coppers didn't pause.

The house had satellite, Curt discovered. He

could tell that the owners hadn't paid their subscription because you couldn't get the sports or the movie channels. There were lots of German stations, but he was crap at German. Still, there was the Cartoon Network and a news channel, both of which were broadcast without encryption. Curt was flicking through the stations when he came across the word "Nottingham" and stopped to have a look.

A couple were giving a press conference, with a senior-looking police officer sitting next to them. She was thirtyish and pretty. He was a lot older and jowly, with bags under his eyes – maybe that was tiredness. Curt recognized the signs. They were the couple whose baby had disappeared. He'd seen the story on the front page of the evening paper.

"We believe that someone out there has got our baby," the woman was saying. "Maybe they took him or maybe they found him. Maybe they can't have a baby of their own. Tom is our only child. We want him back. Please, please return him to us. We don't want you punished, we just want Tom back."

She began to cry. The father spoke next. He, Curt could tell, was not so convinced that the baby was still alive. He didn't appeal to the kidnapper, if kidnapper there was.

"Someone out there must know something. Maybe you're not saying because you don't want to get a friend or close family member into trouble. But please, we need to find Tom. We need to know what's happened to him. There's a number you can ring – anonymously if you like…"

The police superintendent took over, going into ways the public could help. He finished by saying: "If Tom hasn't been found by tomorrow morning, Saturday, we want to undertake a full-scale search of as wide an area as he could have walked or crawled to. This will be supervized by the police, but we don't have the personnel to do such a huge job on our own. So we're asking for volunteers. If you're local and would like to help, please ring the number which will be given in a moment…"

Curt got a pen out of his school bag and wrote the number down. Then he changed the channel to *The Jetsons* and picked up the phone. But he couldn't offer to help, he realized. The police would be looking for him, too.

7

"The records show nothing suspicious about the first Jackson baby's death," Chris told Ruth. "There was no police investigation because it appeared to be a straightforward cot death – but that kind of accidental death's notoriously easy to fake."

"It's still unlikely, though," Ruth commented, as they drove to Louise Jackson's place of work. "So how are we going to ask the ex-wife about it without implying some horrendous scenario?"

"Play it by ear," Chris said. "Only be as direct as we need to be."

They pulled up outside Jackson Associates, Financial Advisers, a newish building off Castle Boulevard. Louise Jackson, it turned out, ran the company. They were shown into her office, a plush, plant-lined room overlooking the canal. The woman behind the desk was fortyish, running to fat but tall enough to carry it, with thick red hair and a designer suit.

"I can give you ten minutes," she said. "I'm meant to be on my way to Colchester by now."

"Business?" Chris asked, politely.

"Yes, new clients. Important to impress them with punctuality. Drink?" Both declined.

"What is it you want to know?" Louise Jackson asked. She wore no wedding ring, Ruth noticed. Still single? Presumably she kept her married name for professional purposes.

"We're investigating the disappearance of your ex-husband's son," Chris said. "We're talking to people connected to the family to see if they can shed any—"

"We've been divorced for three years," Louise interrupted. "The only contact I have with Tony is when he returns Charlotte after a weekend visit."

"I'm sure you understand," Chris said, "that when a child goes missing, we have to look into every possible avenue, no matter how unlikely or distressing."

"Of course." Louise Jackson sat back and lit a cigarette, then switched on an extractor fan which ensured that the smoke didn't reach Ruth and Chris's side of the desk.

"Did you and your husband use to work together?" Chris asked.

"Yes. We were partners. When we split up, he got the house and car and I got the business, which as you can see, I've since built up."

"Isn't it usually the other way round?" Ruth asked, putting on a naïve voice.

"Left to himself, Tony would have run the business into the ground within a year. I've always been its driving force. I'd put everything into Jackson Associates for ten years. The company went through a rough time before the divorce, but I've turned it round since."

"Why did you divorce?" Ruth asked, when Chris didn't follow up.

"He started … misbehaving."

She said this dismissively, but Ruth thought there was more, and waited. Louise took a deep drag on her cigarette, then spoke again.

"We lost a baby. Cot death. I was very depressed afterwards. That was when he … when he…"

For a moment she lost composure and concentrated on stubbing out the cigarette, even though it was only half smoked.

"Forgive me," Ruth said. "We have to ask – were there any suspicious circumstances surrounding the baby's death? Could your husband have had anything to do with—"

"God, no!" Louise interrupted, angrily. "Haven't

you checked the records? Tony was in Japan when it happened, wining and dining clients. It took him thirty-six hours to get back. I had to deal with everything myself: doctors, police, funeral…"

"I'm sorry," Ruth said, and looked at Chris Dylan.

"Just for our paperwork," Chris said, "could you tell us where you were two days ago, between twelve and two?"

Louise checked her personal organizer. "Lunch with my stockbroker," she said. "London. The Bibendum Oyster Bar, to be precise. Want to know what we had?" she added, facetiously.

"Just your stockbroker's name and number, please," Chris said.

She gave it to him.

"We'll also need to speak to your daughter," Chris said, as Louise lit another cigarette.

"Why?"

"Routine."

"Well, you'll find her at her father's tonight. It's his weekend to have her and she insisted on going, though I'd rather she didn't. He picks her up from the High School after work. I suppose they'll be home by half four."

"Thanks," Chris said, standing.

"I hope you find Tom," Louise said, seeing them out.

"I'll drop you at the station," Chris said to Ruth

in the car, adding, "If it's all right with you, I'd like you to come along for the interview with the daughter later."

"I'd be happy to," Ruth said.

"And maybe we can have that drink after, get a bite to eat," Chris suggested.

"Sorry," Ruth said, "can't. I'm having dinner with Clare and her mum."

"Another time, then. Give my best to Clare. Tell her we miss her in CID. When's she coming back?"

"I've no idea," Ruth said.

Trev called by the house just after four, as the *All New Popeye Show* was about to begin. Curt let him in the back.

"Comfy?" he asked.

"Not bad," Curt said, completely bored by now.

"I've just been by this place I was telling you about. Still empty."

"Is there an alarm?" Curt asked.

"I had a good look around. Couldn't see one." People who had alarms usually made a point of making them highly visible.

"There's a back door. You can barely be seen from the street. Crack the glass a bit, put your hand through, a cinch."

"I guess," Curt said.

"Now's the best time. Just getting dark, but most people aren't back from work."

"I guess."

"Weekend's more dodgy. And the owners might be coming home. So…"

"All right, all right." Curt didn't want to do it, but he owed Trev for finding him this place.

"You've got to do it in the next hour," Trev pressed him, "while I'm alibied."

"I said all right," Curt told him, kitting himself up with a blade, a screwdriver and some sellotape. "I'm on my way."

Tony Jackson's BMW was parked in the double garage alongside the apartment. The garage door was open, so they could see that Jenny Jackson's Rover wasn't there. The door was answered by a girl of twelve or thirteen, blonde and quite pretty, in an unformed way. She was still wearing the blue uniform of the High School.

"You must be Charlotte."

"Yes," the girl said, holding the door only half open. "You are…?"

Ruth explained, showing her warrant card. "Your father knows us," she finished.

"Dad's in the shower."

"Actually, it was you we wanted a word with."

"OK. Come in."

With a girl her age, they should have a parent or responsible adult present, but the father was only a room or two away and Dylan didn't seem bothered.

Ruth started on the questions.

"When did you last see your brother?"

"Half brother," Charlotte corrected her. "It's been four weeks. I was meant to come a fortnight ago, but we had a school trip."

"Were you … are you close to Tom?"

Charlotte gave Ruth a sour look. "*Close?* I love him, if that's what you mean. But he's barely two. He knows a few words, but he can't string a sentence together yet."

"He recognizes you?" Dylan prompted. "He knows who you are?"

"Yes, course. Why do you want to know?"

"Routine questions," Ruth assured her. "We have to know the whereabouts of everybody who was close to Tom on the afternoon that he disappeared. You were at school, I presume."

"Actually no," Charlotte said. "Two days ago I was home, in bed. There's this stomach thing going round. I'd been up puking most of the night."

Funny, Ruth thought. You'd have thought that the mother would have mentioned that.

"You were alone, then?"

"Yes."

"Did you call anybody, see anyone?"

Indignantly, Charlotte shook her head. "You can't seriously think that I…?"

"Of course not," Ruth said. "We just want to eliminate you from our enquiries. Can you tell me what you were doing at the relevant times? Between twelve and two, say."

"I was watching the telly in my bedroom."

"What was on?" Dylan asked.

"I'll check." She went over for the *Radio Times*, which was on top of the beech and glass coffee table.

"From memory, please, if you can," Dylan said.

Without warning, the girl burst into tears. "You don't believe me! How could you think that I—?"

"What the hell's going on?" Tony Jackson had walked into the living room, wearing a towelling dressing gown, his hair wet and his face angry. "Charlotte?"

Chris tried to smooth the situation out. "We were asking your daughter a few questions and she got a little upset."

Now Tony Jackson lost his rag. "You shouldn't be asking her questions without an adult present! I'll get on to your boss, you incompetent—"

"There's no need to get angry," Ruth said, gently. "Charlotte took something the wrong way, that's all. Perhaps you'd like to get dressed, sir."

"Or perhaps *you'd* like to leave!"

Dylan didn't argue, so Ruth said nothing, either. The atmosphere had turned pretty poisonous. They stood their ground.

"Have you got any news?" Tony Jackson said tersely, looking at Dylan.

"We've had a lot of volunteers for the search tomorrow morning."

"I should hope so," Jackson said, ungraciously. "Anything else?"

"No. We'll be on our way." They left without ceremony.

"Charming bloke, isn't he?" Dylan said.

"We upset his daughter."

"Yeah. But don't you think they both over-reacted?"

"A bit, yeah."

"Suspicious?"

"Maybe," Ruth said. At Charlotte's age, she'd burst into tears at the smallest thing.

"Can't see it though," Chris went on. "A twelve-year-old kidnapping a two-year-old. Where would she put him? What would she do with him?"

"It doesn't bear thinking about," Ruth said.

"Going on the search tomorrow?" Chris asked, pulling up outside the station.

"Yes. The boss asked me at the end of the shift."

"See you there then," Chris said, a bit of a twinkle in his eye despite the depressing day they'd had.

In the end, Curt couldn't do it. The house was empty all right, and there was no alarm, but the owners had activated their sensor lights before leaving. The bloody things came on as he approached the back door. They would be on a timer so that they only came on when it was dark – after Trev passed by on his paper round.

Curt was relieved. He could get in there all right, but suppose he couldn't get out? After being stuck in the car when it went in the river a couple of weeks ago, he had a horror of being trapped anywhere. Suppose there was a silent alarm linked to the cop station and they came and surrounded him?

Curt wasn't a virgin when it come to breaking and entering. He'd done a few when he was twelve. But then it was just a game, a dare. He took things as souvenirs, trophies, not to sell on. He'd done a bit of shoplifting, yes, who didn't? He'd been best at twocing (taking cars without the owner's consent). But breaking and entering, that was proper crime, career stuff. Uncle Eddie had warned him once: get other people to do the dirty work. Curt listened to his Uncle Eddie.

Squatting in a house whose owners were in Spain was against the law too. But needs must. Anyway, he hadn't taken anything (unless you counted using their electric). Curt wondered if he dared pop in on Julie for a visit. If the social workers were coming, they'd have been by now. He missed his sister, and Tammy. But he didn't want to risk going there, meeting up with Julie's police boyfriend. He'd ring Natalie instead, see if she fancied sneaking over. Then he'd give Trev a bell, tell him the bad news.

Trev acted hard, but he was probably a soft touch. Curt wasn't going to let the lad push him around.

8

By ten the next morning, Saturday, the police were turning away people who wanted to help with the search. The project was partly a public relations job. There wasn't much real prospect of finding the missing child – two thorough searches of the area had already been made. But the toddler had been gone for three days now, and a sense of panic was growing. Sometimes, you needed to be seen doing something, anything.

So out they went, a hundred people examining every bin and skip, combing the fields around the embankment, looking under every piece of rubble in disused factories and warehouses, fingertip-searching wasteground near the football stadiums and any other place which occurred to the officers coordinating it, one of whom was Neil.

The phone rang and Dylan answered it. He grunted a few times, made a couple of notes, then said, "We'll be there in five." He turned to Neil.

"Somebody's reported a body floating in the river. A baby."

Ruth and Jan were first on the scene. It certainly looked like a baby, partially submerged beneath a tree on the city side of the River Trent, heading towards Wilford. A long stick was all that they needed to pull it in, and an appropriate implement had been sent for.

Ruth and Jan weren't needed to fish for the wretched toddler, but for crowd control. Bystanders were gathering. Gossip was brewing.

"Should never have left the door open. What do you expect, the world the way it is today?"

"Have to feel for them, though, don't you? We've all made mistakes."

"He'll have been taken by someone as can't have their own. That's what always happens. Remember Abi…"

"It'll be one of these ponces, you know – perverts. Did you hear about that bloke as got off on Tuesday? Little boy was too scared to give evidence. A scandal."

"I saw the bloke's photograph. Right normal, he looked."

Then, to Ruth's surprise, voices were lowered.

She couldn't make out the murmured words, but she could read the tone, which was hostile. Surely the parents hadn't turned up? She looked around.

It wasn't the parents. It was Alan Wallace, standing a little farther down the bank, wearing a dark red anorak and grey nondescript trousers. He was looking at the scene with binoculars. One of the bystanders tapped Ruth on the shoulder.

"Is that who I think it is?" he said.

Without thinking, Ruth nodded. Wallace's picture hadn't been in the paper when he was freed, only when he was charged. Many people would have forgotten who he was. But not all.

"Are you going to arrest him?"

"What for?" Ruth asked. "Watching?"

A police van was pulling up. Half-heartedly, Jan asked the crowd to move along, or at least move back. Two plain clothes officers got out, one of them wearing orange waterproofs. Neil Foster had drawn the short straw, or the long stick.

"You might not need to get in," Ruth told him.

And, indeed, with Sergeant Dylan holding on to him, Neil managed to prod the object which might be a baby, pushing it beneath the branch it was caught up in.

"Gently now," Dylan said, as Neil tried to hook it.

"Easiest if I pull in the branch, perhaps," Neil said, "bring the baby with it."

Ruth would have cracked a joke about babies and bathwater, but there were bystanders listening. The public didn't understand the black humour which went with the job. Better to laugh at sick jokes than have to cry because of sick things.

Among the watching crowd, all chat had ceased. Alan Wallace, Ruth saw, had come nearer. Neil pulled. The branch moved towards them.

"How heavy does it feel?" Dylan asked, letting go of Neil.

"Hard to tell."

Ruth saw something. "You've lost it!" she yelled.

Neil swore, then jumped in, stick in hand. Ruth pointed him in the right direction. There was a light rain and the current was strongish. If Neil didn't get it in a moment, they'd have to call out the boats.

"There," she said. "You've nearly ... there! That's it!"

Neil was wading along the edge of the Trent. He must be up to his knees in mud. The object had stopped moving. He pulled it towards him.

"Give me a hand. Gentle, now."

Ruth was nearest and took the pole from him. She pulled it in, until the floating object was alongside Neil. He pulled it out and held it up: a pink plastic doll with one arm and half of its hair missing.

"All right," Jan Hunt told the watchers. "Show's over. Off you go."

Alan Wallace was already leaving, worried, perhaps, that he'd been recognized. He was right to be, Ruth saw. Two of the men who'd been watching were following him. Should she follow, make sure that they didn't...? No. Why the hell should she? People like him deserved whatever was coming to them.

"You need to clean up, lad," Dylan told Neil, then turned to Jan. "Can I borrow your oppo again? I need to speak to the daughter, could do with a woman there."

"Be my guest," Jan said, giving Ruth a quizzical look. The sarge herself was the logical choice of partner for the interview. Her experience might make the difference. Why did Chris want Ruth instead? Maybe because Jan Hunt was Chris Dylan's equal. Ruth got the feeling that Chris liked to be in charge.

With all the police around, Curt ought to stay under cover, but he knew that Social Services didn't work weekends if they could help it, so he was meeting Natalie downtown. First, though, he was going to see if they'd found that kid. He wandered through the Meadows, watching the volunteer teams trawl the streets and side alleys, each led by a uniformed copper. At least while they were doing that they'd be too busy to help take him in.

Curt ended up on the Embankment, looking at the river he'd nearly drowned in a few days before. A small crowd had gathered, but was now breaking up. It looked like the police had taken something out of the Trent.

Curt asked one of the people leaving if they'd found anything.

"Don't ask me," he said.

"Just a doll," a woman told him.

"Oh."

Farther down the river, a man in a red anorak stood still, staring at Curt. It was *Call me Alan* from the other day. The woman who'd just spoken to Curt pointed in his direction.

"You know who he is, don't you?"

"No," Curt said.

"He's that Wallace pervert, just got let out of prison. You want to steer clear of him, son."

"I can look after myself," Curt said, not surprised that the guy was known for doing what he'd tried to do with him. Curt had learnt not to be shy in dealing with blokes like that.

Wallace wasn't the first bloke who'd tried something on with him. One of Mum's boyfriends got into his bed once. Julie had warned him about the guy beforehand – "With people like that, act dim and complain loud. It's the only way." The advice had come in useful more than once since. That first time, Curt ran screaming into Mum's room. She'd soon given the boyfriend the elbow.

Wallace was walking away now, followed by two blokes in denim jackets. Curt could tell that they meant him harm. The police were gone. It wouldn't be long.

The Wallace guy was under the footbridge which went across the Trent when they jumped him. It was an efficient doing over, Curt could see: plenty of blows to the chest and testicles, a few in the face to finish off, then into the river.

The men ran off. Curt had only seen their backs, couldn't have identified them even if he were that way inclined. He watched for a couple of minutes, making sure that Wallace could swim. Not that Curt could have helped him. He'd never learnt. As *Call me Alan* climbed out of the river, Curt walked rapidly away, heading into town to meet Natalie.

"Where is she?" Ruth asked Dylan. They were alone in his car.

"Helping with the search. Wouldn't be very impressive if the family didn't help, now would it?"

"I guess not."

"I want you to have another go with her, help out, see if you can get her to open up."

"You seriously think that she might…"

"I've got a nose for these things," Dylan said,

with a grim smile. "I smelt it yesterday. Something not right there. Maybe the girl's jealous of the attention the new kid's getting from her dad."

"So she killed him?" Ruth said, incredulously. "That's monstrous."

"I hate to tell you this," Dylan said, with his sad smile, "but some people *are* monsters."

They were quiet for a while, driving around the Meadows, looking for Charlotte Jackson.

"How was your evening with Clare?" Dylan asked.

"Fine."

Actually, it had been a downbeat evening, the conversation strained. At one point, Ruth had tried to get Clare talking about Dylan. She seemed to recollect that he had tried it on with her once, when Clare was between boyfriends. But Clare seemed to have forgotten. Maybe that was down to the anti-depressants the doctor had her on. Ruth didn't like the idea of them, but if they got Clare through the night, fair enough.

Ruth said none of this to Chris, who she hardly knew.

"When's Tracey back?" she asked, to make conversation.

"Monday, I think."

So CID would have no further use for Ruth after that. Maybe it was for the best. If Tom Jackson wasn't found by Monday, the story could only have an unhappy ending.

"There she is," Dylan said.

Charlotte Jackson was with her stepmother and half a dozen others, combing the car park of a closed-down pub in between the railway station and London Road. John Farraday was leading the team. He waved at them. Chris drove into the car park and pulled up alongside him.

"Think he might be hiding in the weeds?" Dylan asked, jokily.

Farraday looked affronted. "There's always a chance you'll find an open drain cover, or a dumped car that the kid crawled into and couldn't get out of again."

Dylan smiled. "Right." Both of them knew it was extremely unlikely that Tom Jackson had come this far under his own steam.

"Listen," Dylan said, "we want a word with the daughter. Could you get her over here for us, then keep the mother busy?"

"Sure."

He brought Charlotte to the car. Ruth got out to meet her. Chris let her do the talking.

"I'm sorry we got off on the wrong note yesterday," she said. "Would you like to get out of the cold for a minute or two?"

"Why?" Charlotte, asked, sullenly.

"There are a few things we need to go over. We'll get Jenny over here, if you like."

"No thanks," Charlotte said. "I've seen enough of

her already this morning." She got in. Ruth joined her on the back seat. Charlotte rubbed her hands together to warm them up.

"You and Jenny don't get on?" Ruth asked.

Charlotte hesitated, then said, "She acted all interested at first, until Tom came."

"Must have been a hard time."

"Are your parents divorced?" Charlotte asked the police officer.

"No," Ruth said. She'd be happier if they were.

"Got brothers or sisters?"

"No."

"You don't know anything about it, then."

"Sorry," Ruth said, trying to think of a way to make Charlotte identify with her. In the majority of missing child cases like this one, a family member was involved. Charlotte's mother had a solid alibi (her stockbroker had verified it), but that left three people who hadn't. Charlotte was one of them.

"We need to finish our conversation about Wednesday afternoon," Ruth said. "It's just routine."

"If you say so."

"Did you go to the doctor about your stomach upset?"

"Course not. It was only a twenty-four-hour thing."

"What about your mum?"

"She wrote me a sick note, didn't she?"

"And you didn't see anyone else that day? Someone you weren't meant to see, perhaps? A boyfriend who was skiving off?"

"I'm only twelve and a half," Charlotte said, testily, then turned away to gaze into the distance. "I'm too young to have a boyfriend."

There was something edgy there, Ruth thought. Maybe she'd touched a nerve with the boyfriend business. She pressed her.

"I'll bet that lots of girls in your year have boyfriends."

"Lots of them *pretend* to have all sorts of things."

"I know what you mean," Ruth said, waiting to see what Charlotte said next, which turned out to be nothing. Ruth changed tack. "Have you thought of anything which might help us?" she asked.

"Like what?"

"I don't know. Strange people in the area. Any odd behaviour on Tom's part which might lead you to think…" Ruth let the sentence trail off. She didn't know what Charlotte might be led to think.

"Look, I hadn't seen him for four weeks, all right? Everyone's talking about this pervert that they let out of prison. Maybe it was him, I dunno. But I was in bed all day, watching soaps. I had nothing to do with him going."

She burst into tears. The girl cried easily, or maybe Ruth was saying something particularly upsetting, only she didn't know what it was. She heard Dylan swearing under his breath.

Ruth was making a mess of the interview. She handed Charlotte a tissue. "Sorry," she said. "I didn't meant to upset you. It's just that we have to—"

"You're just doing your job," Charlotte said, sarcastically. "That's what Dad told me the other day. But if you were doing your job properly, you'd have found him by now, wouldn't you?"

"It's not always that easy," Ruth said.

"Instead, all you've come up with is this – this stupid search. It's all pretend, isn't it? Everything's pretend!"

Ruth thought that she was going to burst into tears again, but she didn't.

"Can I go now?" Charlotte asked.

Ruth glanced at Dylan, who nodded. "Yes," she said. "Sorry I upset you."

"What did I do wrong?" Ruth asked the detective when the girl was gone.

"Nothing," he said, with that sad smile. "It's a funny age, early adolescence."

"I get the feeling that there's something not right there," Ruth said, "something she's not telling us. To do with a bloke, perhaps."

"You may be right. Most women's problems are brought about by blokes," Dylan said, adding, jokily, "or so my ex-wife used to tell me."

"So how are we going to find out what it is?" Ruth asked.

"Search me," Dylan said. "Nine times out of ten, we never do."

9

Ben and Gary had both pulled a double shift. The overtime was available because of the missing boy on their beat and also because of what day it was: Hallowe'en. You could expect all kinds of trouble when Hallowe'en fell on a Saturday night.

The search for Tom Jackson had yielded nothing: no clues, no sightings, not even a smelly red herring or two to give them hope. Now Inspector Winter was warning the shift about public panic.

"Kids unaccounted for make people nervous. And tonight we're going to have hundreds on the street, each of them a potential troublemaker, each of them a potential victim. So, after dark, the Chief Constable wants a heavy police presence – all cars out, no sitting around the station waiting for something to happen."

"Are you staying on, boss?" Gary asked.

"I'd love to, but it's the mother-in-law's birthday," Winter said, with a sardonic smile. "Bill Cropper's on."

Cropper supervized the relief after theirs. He was a tyrant of the old school.

"How about you, sarge?" Gary asked Jan. "You staying on?"

"And leave Henry with a childminder for five minutes more than I have to? No thanks," Jan Hunt said. "But seeing as you are, there's a call come in. Remember that paedo who got let out on Tuesday? He's been mugged."

"Oh, tough," Gary said, with mock concern.

"My feelings precisely," Jan said, "and presumably the reaction that he was expecting, as he called his solicitor before calling us. He's at her office: Jagger and Co. Know where to find it?"

Ben grunted an affirmative. He knew who Alan Wallace's solicitor was. That was the last thing he wanted, seeing another ex-girlfriend.

Worse, Charlene Harris was rather more than an ex-girlfriend. She was Ben's first love, the woman he'd expected to marry. They'd been together for five years and he still wasn't quite sure why he'd finished with her.

"You're going to see Charlene?" Neil asked, on his way in as Ben and Gary were on their way out. "I've been trying to get hold of her. Could you ask her something for me? When Wallace isn't around, I mean…"

"Why do you think he's at his solicitor's?" Gary asked five minutes later, as they drove towards Wellington Circus.

"Dunno. Maybe he's afraid we'd beat him up if we saw him alone."

It wasn't Charlene who let them in, but Ian Jagger, her boss, which made Ben feel even worse. Jagger was a racist with far right connections: Ben knew this, but couldn't prove it. He'd tried to persuade Charlene not to work for him, but by then (he was two-timing her with Ruth) she'd stopped believing anything he said.

"Mr Wallace is with our Ms Harris," Jagger said. "I'm only here to make sure that things go smoothly. He's a little paranoid." Jagger smiled, then added, "Which doesn't mean that people aren't out to get him."

Wallace was a pretty standard-looking creep, Ben thought: badly dressed, boring-looking, annoyingly edgy. But put him in the right clothes and he could be a cop or a businessman. You could never tell what people were really like from looking at them. Right now he was shaking – maybe because he'd caught a cold in the river where he'd been dumped earlier, or maybe because he was both scared and indignant.

"They meant to kill me!" he said. "To drown me! If I weren't a strong swimmer…"

"We thought you'd get a police doctor to take a look at him," Charlene said.

"Not on a Saturday," Ben told her. "He'll have to go to casualty if any of his injuries are serious."

In casualty he'd face a wait of five hours, minimum, but Charlene didn't complain. She found this bastard just as distasteful as he did, Ben could tell. Her being here was a waste of time, but Wallace would have insisted on it. Strange, though, that Jagger should come out too. Was Wallace any danger to a grown woman?

"My client wants police protection," Charlene said. "He's scared that his attackers know where he lives, and will follow him there."

"I've had stuff in the letterbox," Wallace said. "Excrement, razor blades…"

"Then I advise you to be vigilant," Ben said. "But we can't offer you protection. Even with the best will in the world, tonight's Hallowe'en and we've got a missing child on our hands. The most I can do is ask the patrol cars to keep an eye open. They'll be out in force tonight."

The conversation dribbled on but Wallace wrung no more concessions from them. Ben couldn't see why he'd bothered to report the crime. He hadn't seen his assailants properly. According to him, there'd been plenty of witnesses about, but nobody had reported it, nobody had come forward to help him. It was unlikely that any witness would show up now. Best bet, Ben knew, was that the attackers were friends or members of the families of the children Wallace had abused. He couldn't see CID wanting to investigate them too closely.

After a few minutes, Wallace calmed down, as if becoming aware that everybody there thought he'd got less than he deserved.

"Gary, would you see Mr Wallace out?" Ben asked. "I need a couple of minutes with Ms Harris."

"Sure."

It was the first time they'd been alone in a room together for months. Ben couldn't remember the last occasion. Charlene looked beautiful, if flustered. But he didn't have any mad pangs of regret. Nor, from the looks of her, did she.

"Thanks for getting him out of the way like that," she said. "He gives me the creeps. Was there really something you wanted?"

"Not me, but Neil," Ben said. "About this missing child. No one really thinks your man was involved. The kid's too young. But his alibi is that he was here on Wednesday afternoon, when the boy vanished."

"Yes," Charlene said. "He was." She checked her diary. "But not until four. I had to squeeze him in at the end of the day. Does that mean…"

Ben shrugged. "It means he could have done it,

yes. But if he had, I hardly think he'd be calling us out, or watching us search the river, do you?"

"I guess not," Charlene said. "Good. He's one client I'd be happy to lose. I don't want him committing any new crimes."

There was an awkward pause which Ben eventually broke by saying, "How are you?"

"Well," she said. "You?"

"Fine."

"And Ruth? How's that going?"

"Gone."

"Oh." She pursed her lips in an expression he knew. It was not quite a smile.

Ben could have asked about her love life then, but didn't. Suppose she were single? He would have to explain that he wasn't and then she would have to make it clear that he was the last person on earth who she would want to go out with. Though they both knew that wasn't true.

"Can we give you a lift home?" he offered.

"No thanks," she said. "Ian's taking me."

"Of course, right."

Charlene lived quite near her boss, who had a posh apartment in the Park. One day, Ben thought, she'll see through him, and be out of this place like a shot.

"See you then," he said. "Take care."

"And you."

A surprisingly civilized encounter, Ben thought, as they drove away. He wondered if it would ever be like that with Ruth. Not while they were working together, that was for sure.

Curt was dozing when Trevor came round the back, making so much noise he was worried the neighbours would hear. Curt let him in. It was two in the afternoon (Trev did his paper round earlier on Saturdays). Broad daylight. Curt had been hoping to be gone before the youth showed up.

"Are you trying to get me caught?" Curt complained.

"No one in next door," Trev smirked. "How'd you go on yesterday?"

Curt explained.

"You were put off by a poxy light!" Trev complained.

"It was a powerful security light," Curt protested. "I'd have been seen."

"Bollocks!"

"Go and do it yourself if you think it's so easy."

"I'm their paper boy, idiot! Someone might recognize me."

"Don't call me an idiot!"

All right, Curt might be in a bottom group for every setted subject at school, but that was because he'd missed so much time, not because he was thick.

"Anyway," he added, "I live round here, too, remember."

"All right," Trev said, reluctantly, "I'll tell you what. There's this other place. They've not had papers since last Sunday, so I reckon they're away until tomorrow, maybe another week."

"Can't you sneak a look at the order book?" Curt asked.

"Terry Simons don't leave it open that often. Anyway, go in today, and you're bound to be all right. I had a look inside this place last Christmas, when I collected my tip. Simple lock. No alarm or any of that crap. And they're dead well-off. Gave me a fiver."

"So why do you want me to rob them, then?"

"They can afford it, can't they? They'll have insurance."

"I'm not sure," Curt said. "Not today, definite. I'm meeting Natalie, staying over at hers tonight. If they don't have a paper tomorrow, I'll take a look."

"Wait until dark and do it this aft'," Trev ordered.

Curt told him where to go.

"I found you this place," Trev reminded him.

"I'll find another if I need to. And remember, *you're* not taking any risks. If I get caught doing stuff again, I go down until I'm eighteen."

"Everybody told me you were hard," Trev said.

"And you thought that meant I was thick, too?" Curt snapped. "Best I can do, give me the address. I'll take a look in daylight before I go to Nat's."

"All right," Trev said. "But you're not going to go in then cut me out, are you?"

"We've got a deal," Curt said.

"And you'll sort out transport – nick a car?"

"Yeah."

"Good stuff," Trev said, looking more comfortable.

The deal was that Curt and Trevor would split the proceeds down the middle. Curt knew that the youth would never give him half – a third, maybe, if he was lucky. However, if Curt did the job he would hold back from giving Trev the best stuff. If there was any cash or decent jewellery, he'd stash it for later. That was something else his Uncle Eddie had drummed into him: there was no honour among thieves. Take what you can and hide it well.

"Now then," said Curt, "what's the address?"

Trev told him. "Aren't you going to write it down?"

"I've got a memory," Curt said, raising his voice.

Before Trev could reply, there was a loud rap on the door. It sounded almost official.

"You idiot!" Curt hissed at Trev. "You were seen."

"Me?" Trev hissed back. "You were the one shouting just now."

"I know you're in there!" a voice yelled. "Open this door!"

Trev swore. "I'm off."

Without waiting for Curt, he did a runner out the

back. Curt didn't know what to do. He'd been sleeping on a bed upstairs. Now he ran up there, took a look out of the window. It was an old bloke, not the police. Probably the neighbour who Trev said was out. Curt threw his stuff into the knapsack he used for school, then looked out of the window again.

"You won't get away!" the old bloke was yelling. He must have seen Trev as he came out of the back alley on to the street. The bloke began running after him. Curt prayed that Trev didn't get caught. He would give up Curt in the blink of an eye.

At least Curt had a couple of minutes' grace. He tidied the bed, looked around for traces of himself, found none. He'd been careful. Downstairs, he turned the electric back off, then let himself out quietly through the back. He exited the alley from the other end, making sure that the street was clear first. He was on the embankment before he heard the first siren. With any luck, the police would think that the old bloke had imagined the break in. He'd got away with it again.

Not dark yet. In the parade room, Gary was waiting for Ben. Ruth was waiting to be partnered before they all went out and did their high profile Hallowe'en bit. Then Chris Dylan came over.

"Got to do some callbacks at the Riverside Estate," Chris told Ruth. "Want to give me a hand?"

"Still need a woman's touch?" Ruth asked, half flirting with him.

Dylan smiled. "You said it."

"You'll have to OK it with Inspector Cropper."

"Sure."

As Dylan went off in search of the Inspector, the phone rang. Gary answered. It was a woman with a northern accent.

"Is Ruth Clarke there, please?" She sounded upset.

'Yes," Gary said, signalling to Ruth. "Who's calling?"

"Her mother."

"Hold on," he covered the mouthpiece and passed the phone to Ruth. "Your mum."

"You're kidding!" Ruth said, eyes widening.

"No. Want some privacy?"

Ruth nodded. Gary went to use the photocopier. Dylan nearly bumped into him on his way back. Gary told the sergeant to give Ruth a minute. "Personal call."

"Got a new boyfriend, has she?" Dylan asked. Gary noted his curiosity.

"No," he replied. "Family stuff."

"Right."

Dylan stood awkwardly, waiting. It was no secret in the station that Gary was gay, but most officers pretended not to know. Dylan had never mentioned it. Even so, Gary could tell that it made him uncomfortable. In such situations, he almost always tried to break the ice.

"Ruth's helping you out, is she?" he asked.

"S'right," Dylan said. "You know, you could do worse than take after her. She's solid. Thinks too. You share digs with her and Clare, don't you?"

"That's right."

"There's a lot of blokes who'd pay a lot of money to change places with you."

Gary grinned. "Including you, eh?"

For a moment, he thought he'd gone too far, but then Dylan winked. They'd established some kind of *camaraderie*. Gary would have to tell Ruth that he was interested, but he didn't get the chance. She came out of the parade room and spoke to Dylan.

"I just need a wee, then I'm ready to go."

"Take your time," the DS said. "Everything all right?"

"Fine."

"Family crisis averted," Dylan commented when she was gone.

"Looks like it," Gary said, as Ben returned with their lunch.

Dylan blanked the black copper completely.

"Tell her I'm waiting in the car," the DS said, and left.

His attitude to Ben did not go unobserved. Gary's partner raised his eyebrows in mild disdain. "Seen Neil around?" he asked.

"Still finishing off the search," Gary told him, as Ben handed over his roast beef and coleslaw roll.

"Any joy?"

"Not a jot."

"The kid's a goner, isn't he?" Ben said.

It was a rhetorical question. There was no need for Gary to reply and they both knew what his answer would have been.

"Come on," Ben said. "Let's go and make the streets safe for all those little beggars in masks."

10

Neil got the call from Ben as the search was winding up. In the windy station car park, Inspector Cropper was thanking the crowd of helpers.

"We haven't found Tom Jackson, but we have come up with a lot of information, some of which may yet help us to locate him. Most importantly, we know where he *isn't* and can redirect our efforts accordingly. On behalf of the Chief Constable and the Jackson family, may I offer you all our hearty thanks."

Complete cobblers, Neil knew. In truth, the inspector was annoyed about how little success they'd had, while the Jacksons were on the verge of giving up hope.

Neil was going to call Dylan but saw DI Greasby first. The DI was liaising with Major Crimes, and therefore a more appropriate person to talk to than Dylan.

"That paedo who was let out Tuesday, sir. I've had his alibi checked, and it seems that he joined his solicitor rather later than he led us to believe."

"Interesting," Greasby said.

"He hadn't got an alibi for the relevant times as it was, but if he lied, it might be significant."

"You're right," Greasby said. "Go and see him, but clear it with Major Crimes first. They're covering the paedophile angle."

"Have they come up with anything good?" Neil asked the DI.

"Not a lot. The Sex Offenders Register has been gone over with a fine-toothed comb, but it's bugger all use."

The Sex Offenders Register covered sexual offenders (75 per cent of whom were paedophiles) who'd been convicted or released under licence since September 1st, 1997. So it didn't contain people like Alan Wallace, whose only conviction was earlier. Nor did it cover people who'd been cautioned, had charges dropped, or whom the police were particularly suspicious of. That was why Notts had its own computer database for tracking paedophiles. Even so, experts reckoned that only ten per cent of paedophiles ever came to police attention.

"Why's that?" Neil asked.

"The trouble with the database is that there's so much material that's its hard to prioritize. Also, sexual abuse of two-years-olds is pretty rare. And, when it happens, it almost always happens in families. So Wallace probably isn't our man. Did I hear someone say that the council placed him opposite a nursery school?"

"S'right."

"Then it better not be him, or there'll be hell to pay!"

The bell took a while to be answered, which was often a sign of someone hiding something. The explanation turned out to be simpler, though: *West Side Story*, turned up very high. Chris and Ruth could only hear it when Jeremy Tate opened the door. He let them into the porch area and left them there.

"I've already been questioned twice," he complained, when he'd turned his CD off. "I'm in the middle of my ironing, then I have a work meeting. This is really terribly inconvenient."

"What work is it you do, sir?" Dylan asked, playing innocent. He'd read the files, been at the briefing, knew that Tate was a middle-aged home worker with no criminal record.

"I'm an accountant."

"And you have no recollection of ever having seen Tom Jackson?"

"No," Tate said, smiling unctuously. "I'm not very child friendly. I don't tend to look closely at the little monsters. Not that I mean that this boy was … I'm sorry."

Dylan looked at Ruth, who was preoccupied, but roused herself.

"You like animals though, don't you?" she said.

"Not especially."

"Only I noticed your cat." She pointed at the white animal, which was rubbing itself against Dylan's ankle. "Children like cats, too," she added. "Maybe…"

"Horatio's not mine," Tate told her. "He belongs to some friends – more neighbours, really. I said I'd pop into their place and feed him while they were on holiday, but he seems to have adopted me – prefers my leftovers to cat food."

He talked in a melodious, slightly self-conscious way. Ruth was ninety per cent sure that he was gay. Living with Gary had made her sensitive to the pointers.

"If you think of anything, sir," she said, "please call us."

"I'll do that. Horatio, get off him!"

The cat – more of a kitten, really, it couldn't eat much – scurried away, to Dylan's relief.

"What do you think?" he asked, as they continued to walk around the estate.

"Not likely," Ruth said. "You know, I think we're

barking up the wrong tree, targetting sad, middle-aged men who may or may not be sexually interested in children. With a child Tom's age, isn't it more likely that a woman's taken him – say, someone who can't have kids of their own, or who's lost her own child?"

"Makes sense," Chris told her, "but that kind of thing doesn't happen often. When it does, the cases get a lot of publicity and there's a spate of copycat crimes, so they seem more common. Thing is, it's very hard to conceal a baby, so you have to have a very good story. With the amount of publicity about Tom Jackson, we've had a few calls. But they're either cranks who want to settle a score, or there's a simple explanation: relatives visiting, kids who've been legally adopted and so on."

"Just a thought," Ruth said.

"Are you all right? You've been looking a bit down since we came out."

"Nothing that a few gins and a decent meal to-night won't cure."

"Fair enough," Chris said. "I'm buying. That is, if you'll let me."

Ruth didn't have to think for long. Sam and Clare were still away and Gary was going round to Umberto's. "All right," she said. "I'd like that."

"Pick you up at eight. Taxi job. We'll go somewhere nice."

"Brilliant."

"Come on, then," he said. "Better see if the occupants of number nineteen have returned."

The Riverside Estate wasn't Curt's kind of stamping ground. He didn't feel comfortable in places as posh as this. Back when he'd done a few break-ins, it had been terraced houses or first-floor maisonettes, not these fancy house-cum-flat complexes where, for all he knew, they might have a video camera trained on you. Back then, he used to do it with a mate, for a laugh. *Creeping*, they called it. The biggest thrill was to go into a place when the occupants were in and watch them watching the telly, or doing the ironing, whatever.

One time, though, he got caught, full police caution job. No one believed him when he said that he wasn't there to nick things, that he only ever took something as a souvenir. Mum beat the crap out of him when she got him home. So, thinking about it now, Curt decided he was owed a successful burglary, to make up for the one he'd not done but been punished for.

Number nineteen, Riverside Close, was on a corner, so only overlooked on one side. Curt watched as a couple came out of the place next door. It looked like the houses had porches, so there were probably two doors to get through. Get in through the first and you could take your time with the second, which was OK. The people from number seventeen were going into number nineteen. So much for Trev saying it was empty! But no, they were only ringing the doorbell. And those drawn curtains gave it away. Trev said there was a light left on inside, which only showed after dark. Convenient, that, as it meant Curt didn't have to worry about a torch beam being spotted.

The people at the door were coming away. *Police*, he could tell at a glance. The bloke had a definite look of CID: square jaw, cheap suit, shifty eyes. The woman was ten years younger and small, for a plonk. She looked more like a schoolteacher. What were they doing here? Was someone else already working these buildings? Curt didn't want to run into a professional on a job. That had happened to his mate, Joe, and it had nearly cost him his life.

Then Curt remembered: this was where the missing kid went from. He'd seen the place on the news. It felt wrong. *Sod it!* he thought. *I don't need to do this*. He was staying at Nat's tonight. Tomorrow, he'd find somewhere else to stay, somewhere he didn't owe to Trevor. He'd make a new plan, one that didn't involve burglary or being in a children's home.

If push came to shove he could talk to one of the homeless selling *The Big Issue*, see if they knew of somewhere. If he lied about his age, Curt could sell papers too, he supposed, though it was getting too cold to live on the streets. *This is all thanks to my mum*, he reminded himself. *Well, I hope you're finally having a good time, Mum, wherever you are, 'cos I'm having a crap one.*

"Have you caught them?" Alan Wallace asked, as Neil sat down on a bumpy, threadbare armchair which faced the window.

"Caught who?" Neil asked.

"The bastards who put me in the river this morning."

Neil had almost forgotten about that. "Sorry", he said, "not my department."

"What do you want, then?" Wallace asked, uneasily.

"It's about Wednesday afternoon. You told one of my colleagues that you were at your solicitor's. What time was that?"

"Can't say as I remember," Wallace replied, his expression filling with suspicion.

"Let me refresh your memory," Neil said. "According to the appointment book at Jagger and Co, you were there at four in the afternoon."

"If that's what it says, it must be right."

"We need to know what you were doing in the three hours before that."

Wallace thought for a moment, hooded lids half covering his eyes.

"I went into town a bit earlier, walked round the shops a bit."

"How about before that – between, say, twelve-thirty and two?"

Tom Jackson had gone missing between one and half-past.

"I was here."

"Alone?" Neil asked.

There was a slight hesitation before Wallace replied with a monosyllabic "yeah".

"Did anyone call, anyone who can verify your presence?"

Again, Wallace hesitated. Then, "Why are you asking me this?"

"You know about the child who went missing," Neil said, gently.

"I'm not into two-year-olds."

"I didn't say you were. But we need to eliminate you from our enquiries."

"So what have I got to do?" Wallace asked, in a wheedling tone. "Make sure I've got an alibi for every minute of the day in case a child goes missing?"

Neil didn't answer this. Instead, he said, "We've had several phone calls from people suggesting that you might have been involved in the toddler's disappearance."

"People have got it in for me."

"Doubtless."

They'd reached a standoff. Alan Wallace was staring calmly at Neil, his whole body still except for the feet, which took turns to tap against the carpet, impatiently. Neil suspected that he was going to give something up.

Then the doorbell rang.

"Expecting someone?" Neil asked.

Wallace shook his head. "But I know what it'll be."

He went into the kitchen area to get something. Neil stood up and looked out of the window. Kids – aged eight or nine, by the size of them. One had a tall witch's hat, with cape and broom. The other wore some kind of green ghoul mask, which he or she was lighting from underneath with a torch. Without consulting Neil, Wallace came out of the kitchen and went downstairs.

What kind of parents let their children come to a place like this, full of single men, several of whom had recently been in prison? Probably they didn't know the kids were here. But where was the parent, the older brother or sister who should be supervising them? Didn't they know this world was not a safe place?

Downstairs, the door opened.

"Trick or treat!" the kids yelled.

Neil couldn't hear Wallace's reply, but the kids were all "Thanks, mister!" Neil wasn't worried. Wallace wouldn't do anything with him around. But what about later? He took a quick look in the kitchen. There, on the table, was a cardboard box containing mini Mars bars, lollipops and Love Hearts. What was to stop him, when Neil was gone, from inviting a kid upstairs if they wanted a little more?

The paedophile returned with a smile on his face which made Neil sick to his stomach. Unprofessionally, he lashed out.

"I'll bet this is your favourite day of the year," he sneered.

Wallace went to a cupboard, got out a cheap bottle of supermarket whiskey, then poured a couple of centimetres into a wide glass. "Actually," he said, after drinking half, "it's torture."

Neil wanted to leave, but there was something which Wallace wasn't telling him, and maybe the booze would loosen his tongue.

"Tell me about it," Neil said, reverting to a friendly tone.

Wallace finished the drink in two sips and poured another, larger one.

"I like children," he said.

"Right," Neil said, non-judgementally.

"It's an illness, if you like – a condition. I can't help it."

Neil didn't buy that, but tried to be sympathetic. He wanted Wallace on his side.

"Someone did something to you when you were young, perhaps?"

"No!" Wallace asserted, his voice louder. "I'm

not making excuses. It's my nature. Got that? It's the way I am."

"I see."

"No, you don't. Imagine, for a moment – I don't suppose you've got much imagination, but try – you're in a world where sex with women is outlawed, where society says that all sex must take place between people of the same sex and anything else is unnatural. What would you do?"

It was a stupid scenario, Neil thought, but he played along.

"I don't know. Be celibate, I guess."

"But all around you, there are women who want you, women who are curious about sex, women who are gagging for it. And there's not much risk that you'll be caught. What do you do now?"

"It's not the same," Neil argued. "Kids only do what you ask because they're used to doing what adults tell them to. They're afraid. They don't really want to."

"How do you know? What's wrong with kids being curious about sex?"

He believed it, Neil saw. Here was an intelligent man, a former primary school teacher, who had convinced himself that children wanted what he wanted. It disgusted him, but he was trained to hide his feelings.

"Kids are curious about everything," Neil said. "But that doesn't mean—"

"Oh, forget it," Wallace whined. "People like you will never understand. But put yourself in my position. I can't do the one job I really love, working with children, and I can't have the only kind of sexual relationship which I want, either. Not much of a prospect, is it?"

"There are treatments," Neil said.

"I'm going on a *course*," Wallace said, dismissively. "To help me cope. It's in *modules*: antecedents, behaviour, consequences. I know the score. I've been on one before. But there's no cure. I am what I am. You want to know what I was doing between twelve-thirty and two on Wednesday? All right, I'll tell you. There was a lad, hiding from the rain. I invited him up here, gave him a drink, offered to show him a video."

"How old was he?" Neil asked.

"Said he was fifteen, but looked younger to me."

That still made him beneath the age of consent. "Go on," Neil said.

"I tried it on. Nothing happened He wasn't interested. He left."

"What time was this?"

"The boy came up about – oh, ten past one. Left at twenty-five past, maybe."

The alibi covered almost the entire period during which Tom Jackson went missing. There would have been no room for Wallace to get to or from the Riverside Estate in the time left over. If Wallace was telling the truth, it was good enough.

"Do you have a name for this boy?"

"Curt, with a 'c'. I asked."

"Describe him to me."

"Five four or five, short, dark hair, brown eyes, thinnish, vulnerable-looking."

"Wearing?"

Wallace described the uniform of a school up the road. The boy would have been skiving off. Curt wasn't that common a name. It would be fairly easy to track the lad down, if he existed: just visit the school and go through their year lists. Julie Wilder's brother was called Curt, Neil remembered. Which school did he go to?

"All right," Neil said, "I'll check that out."

"He'll probably lie about it," Wallace said, "but nothing happened. I like them younger, as you know. He would have been a compromise."

Neil got up to go.

"You see," Wallace added, "I do try to restrain myself."

"Only because you don't want to get caught," Neil said, reaching for the door handle.

"That's right," Wallace replied. "Fear is a deterrent. Do you want me to tell you about all the things that were done to me while I was inside on remand?"

"Not really," Neil said, as the doorbell rang again. "Don't worry. I'll answer that."

He hurried down the stairs. There were a bunch of dressed-up kids – all ten, eleven, he reckoned – ringing the bell for every room. Neil pulled out his warrant card.

"Police," he said. "Listen, there are some pretty dodgy people living here. *Bogeymen* – know what I mean?"

The children nodded soberly. Neil couldn't see their expressions because of their masks.

"Have you got an adult with you?" he asked. Small heads shook.

"Then I think you'd better clear off. And be careful. There are a lot of funny people around."

"Yes, sir!" said the tallest one. They turned tail and ran off, just as a middle-aged man came down the stairs, wearing a tracksuit and holding some chocolate bars.

"Trick or treat?" he asked Neil.

"S'right. I got rid of them."

There was disappointment on his face. "Pity. I wanted to give them these. I've been here four years, you know. Not many children call here."

When Neil said nothing, he continued to talk. "I had two of my own, once. Died in a fire. Smoke. I carried them out myself. Lost my wife two years later. She never got over it. Gave up then. That's how I ended up here."

"I'm sorry to hear it," Neil said, but his policeman's scepticism was coming into play. Maybe this sob story was designed to deflect him from the man's real intention, which was to interfere with those children.

"Live here, do you? Or just visiting?"

"Just visiting," Neil said. "Actually, I'm running late. Got to go."

"Take care."

A kind man, Neil guessed, prematurely aged by the terrors life had thrown at him. Why had he suspected him? That was what the job did to you. Everybody had a sob story, an excuse. *To understand everything is to forgive everything*, Clare had announced one night when they were discussing some old cobblers about the ethics of law and order. But Neil had never believed that. People knew right from wrong and most of them acted accordingly, most of the time. Those who didn't act that way were bad 'uns, and deserved to be punished.

Neil thought about standing outside the gates of Villiers House, turning away any kids who tried to visit. But he wasn't in uniform, and might be taken for a pervert himself. So, instead, he drove to the station, signed off, then went home. He didn't have any sweets, he remembered, as he pulled up outside his dark, empty house. Kids were bound to call. So he went to the corner shop and bought some.

11

"Thanks for your help," Dylan said.

It was dark now. The Forest match was long over and the shops had shut. All of the occupants of the Riverside Estate who were coming home had come home. Ruth and Chris had reinterviewed as many as they could find of the ones on their list.

"Run you home?" the DS offered.

"I'm meant to be on until seven," Ruth told him.

"To the station, then?"

"Actually, I think I'll walk. There's something I have to think through."

"That phone call earlier?" Dylan asked, tenderly.

"To do with that, yes."

"All right. Be careful, though, won't you?"

"I will."

Ruth knew what Dylan meant, but wasn't saying. Out of uniform, not accompanied by a beefy bloke, she looked like a natural victim: a small woman, on her own in one of the roughest parts of the city.

But Ruth wasn't afraid of much. Instead of heading back towards the city, she walked to the river which glistened behind the estate. Only a high hedge stopped a child from running straight from the back lawns into the Trent. Would the boy's body be washed up on the river's bank one day? It was a strong possibility.

Ruth stopped thinking about Tom Jackson and thought instead about her father, whom she hadn't seen since the previous Christmas, and then only briefly. The phone call this afternoon had been about him.

"A heart attack," her mother had said. "The doctors say it nearly killed him. He's in the Royal Infirmary."

She'd expected Ruth to drop everything, come straight away. All Ruth could think to say was "sorry". She meant sorry for Mum. Many a time she'd wished her father dead. Now she didn't know what she thought, how she felt.

"He might not survive the weekend," Mum told her.

"I see."

There was another conversation going on, one not carried by the telephone lines. *Can't you forgive him?* Mum was asking. And Ruth was saying, *No.* Maybe, if Mum had really gone to town on the emotional blackmail, she would have succumbed: *Don't come for him, come for me.* That might have done it. But Ruth's mother was a proud woman, a trait she'd passed on to Ruth. Mum was always distant, even with her only child. It felt like she was constantly reminding Ruth that other people were never really knowable. When you got right down to it, even your own family would always be strangers.

One time, when Ruth was fourteen or fifteen, she asked her mum why she'd never had any more children. Mum gave her a look like she'd farted in church. What would it have been like to have a brother or sister? Ruth wondered. She'd day-dreamed about stuff like that all the time when she was a kid. But daydreams were best left behind, as was home.

Ruth looked at her watch: nearly seven. She should be on her way by now. She wiped her eyes, blew her nose and turned round, nearly bumping into the twelve-year-old girl who must have been watching her, silently, for some time. She flinched.

"Are you all right?" Charlotte Jackson asked.

"I think so," Ruth said. Then she added, "What are you doing here?"

"I come here sometimes when I'm staying with my dad."

"I guess it's pretty heavy in there at the moment," Ruth commented.

"You're telling me," Charlotte said, sounding more relaxed than earlier. "I stay in my room a lot, but it's not like *my* room – just a spare bedroom. I like looking at the river."

"Me too," Ruth said. "You want to be careful though. There's not much lighting here. Someone could…"

Charlotte reached into her pocket and pulled out a personal safety alarm.

"Good idea," Ruth said.

"You carry one?"

"When I'm off duty, yes."

"So you're on duty now?"

Ruth looked at her watch. "For another two minutes."

Charlotte stared at the river. She was staring so hard, Ruth thought she might be trying to stop it from flowing.

"Is there something you want to tell me?" Ruth asked, after two minutes had passed.

"No," the girl said, firmly.

They stood in silence for a little longer. In the houses behind, a group of children in costume were making their way from door to door, trick or treating. One of their fathers was standing a few steps behind them. When they got to 12A, Charlotte's place, the father told them not to knock, to move on. Ruth looked at her watch. She would never be ready for Chris on time.

"Do you want to walk a little?" she suggested to Charlotte.

"All right."

It was a clear night. Away from the city lights, a few stars were visible.

"Your dad won't be worried?" Ruth asked. "I don't want to..."

"He doesn't tell me what to do."

They left the Trent and walked by the canal.

"Why were you crying before?" Charlotte asked Ruth.

"My father had a heart attack. He's very ill."

Another awkward pause. Charlotte broke it. "I don't understand," she said. "Why aren't you with him?"

Ruth began to walk faster. "We don't get on," she replied.

"Why?"

Ruth didn't believe in telling lies to children, didn't believe in scaring them, either. So what should she say? She didn't know how to tell someone. The one time she had, she ended up wishing that she hadn't.

"He hurt me," she said, finally. "In lots of ways. He let me down."

"Oh," Charlotte said, and nodded as though she understood.

"But if he's dying," Ruth went on, "maybe I ought to forgive him. If I don't, I might never forgive myself."

"You should go," Charlotte said.

Their eyes met and something was exchanged. Some kind of sadness. Ruth couldn't put it into words.

"You're right," Ruth told Charlotte. "But I don't know if I can."

Somehow, without discussing it, they had turned around and were heading back towards the Riverside Estate. In the distance, someone was setting off fireworks.

"Do you know anything about what happened to Tom?" Ruth asked. "Maybe something that you've been afraid to say?"

"I haven't got anything to tell you," Charlotte said. "I wish I had."

Why then, did Ruth get the feeling that Charlotte was holding something back? She reached into her handbag, scribbled her phone number on a bit of paper and gave it to the girl.

"If you want to talk," she said. "I work funny shifts, but I'm often there."

"Thanks," Charlotte said. "I hope…"

She reached out and, in an oddly formal gesture, shook Ruth's hand. Her face was trying to smile, but failing. Her long hair fell shapelessly back behind her ears, making her look strangely angular. Ruth could see the face of the woman she would become. Charlotte already seemed older than Ruth would ever be.

She walked away, a matchstick of a child in a light blue anorak which was far too big for her, a girl who'd lost first one younger brother, then the other. Ruth knew what she ought to do, but instead she walked to London Road and hailed a taxi home. Chris Dylan was picking her up in thirty minutes' time.

The final group of trick or treaters rang just one doorbell at Villiers House, Alan Wallace's. He hurried downstairs, sweets in hand, and was surprised to see only one child in the hallway – a boy, wearing a Herman Munster mask. He looked a bit old to be doing this, but maybe he was tall for his age.

"Trick or treat?" the boy shouted in a nervous, whiny sort of way.

"Oh, treat definitely," Alan said, and held out a mini Mars bar.

Then, despite what he'd said earlier about resisting his urges, he was tempted to go a little further, give it a try.

"Actually," he said, "it's getting late. I'll bet you're the last of the evening. I've got quite a few sweets left. Would you like to come up and choose some more?"

Nervously, the lad nodded his head. Wallace reached out his hand.

"It's just up one flight of stairs," he said, reassuringly. "Come with me."

The boy put a slender hand in his. A shiver of excitement ran through Wallace's body as they walked up the stairs together.

12

"Seven years," Melanie said. "It's not that much, is it? With good behaviour, taking into account the time served, he'll be out in three or four. But Marie and Lorraine are serving a life sentence."

She'd spent the day with two friends who'd been attacked during the summer. Neil had helped to catch the rapist, who, it turned out, they both knew.

"At least he was convicted," Neil said. "Life won't be easy for him in prison. Even when he's released, the conviction will follow him round for the rest of his life. He'll be on the Sex Offenders Register. Whereas this guy I saw today, Wallace, won't be. The things he did to those kids and he doesn't even have to answer for them in court, never mind face a jury of his peers."

He stopped. Melanie was looking askance at him. Sometimes she got fed up when he talked about work. Her eyes glazed over, the way his did when she got carried away talking about some poet she liked, or a play.

"Marie and Lorraine are my friends," she said. "This Wallace bloke is work. Do you always have to dump those nightmares on me?"

"Sorry," he said. "Tell me more about your day."

But Melanie changed the subject. "There's a party," she said, "in Lenton. Marie told me about it. Someone I know, a third-year, so we won't be gatecrashing. I thought we could head into town in half an hour or so, have a drink or go to a movie. Then go on to the party after."

"I guess."

Neil had been planning on a long bath, followed by a takeout, a few cans, and a video if there was nothing good on TV.

"I'll get some food then. What do you fancy? Pizza, or fish and chips?"

"Er ... fish," Neil said. "Haddock. I think I'll grab a quick shower while you're away."

"Don't be too long in there," she said, reverting now to her cheeriest tone because she'd got her way with their evening plans. "I know what you're like."

She kissed him on the cheek, borrowed a fiver and the *Evening Post* to check what films were on, and went out. As Neil went upstairs, the doorbell rang. More trick or treaters, probably, but he didn't have time to deal with them.

Sometimes the best way to handle problems is to get wrapped up in someone else's. Ruth lay in the bath, thinking about Louise and Charlotte Jackson. Each of them, she'd felt, had been holding something back. But what? She juggled the events of the last week in her mind, ignoring, for once, the terrible fear of tragedy which overwhelmed everyone when a child went missing. Ruth suspected abuse of some kind: probably the father, just possibly the step-mother. But if Charlotte had been trying to tell her that, Ruth would have read the signals. Wouldn't she?

Suddenly, in a flash, it came to her. Mother and daughter were in league. Charlotte had kidnapped Tom, then her mother had hidden him until the fuss died down. Earlier, when Charlotte told Ruth that she didn't know where Tom was and wished that she did, it was the literal truth. But Louise would know. She and her daughter had taken Tom, in one fell swoop getting revenge against Tony Jackson for betraying them by leaving, as well as a replacement for the baby brother who had died.

Keeping such a thing secret would be difficult, but Louise Jackson was wealthy. She had the money to get around most of the obvious pitfalls. False documents could be bought. A fake father would appear on the birth certificate, unless a friend or lover volunteered for the role. A private, boarding school education could be managed discreetly. As long as nobody suspected what they'd done, the subterfuge could work.

No wonder Charlotte looked miserable. She didn't like her father and hated her stepmother, but had to see them often. She would withdraw very slowly from their lives so as not to draw suspicion on herself and her mother. Sooner or later, perhaps when Jenny got pregnant again (presuming she did), Charlotte would drop her dad completely, returning to the bosom of her mother and half brother.

Was the idea far-fetched? Ridiculously. But you read more bizarre things in the Sunday papers. Ruth would try it out on Chris tonight, after a few drinks. Damn! she thought. Chris! What time did he say he'd come? No time to wash her hair. She got out of the bath and was still towelling herself off when the doorbell rang. There was nobody else in the house to answer it. Ruth put on a dressing gown and went downstairs to let him in, well aware what signal she was sending out.

"Sorry," she told him, accepting the bunch of carnations he thrust at her. "I was held up earlier. I won't be long though."

"No worries."

She ushered him into the kitchen, gave instructions

for the making of drinks, and put the flowers in water. It was a long time since Ben had brought her flowers. If she had been thinking that tonight was just a case of two single people getting together to mull over work, she would have to think again. But she hadn't been thinking, not really. She'd been making up silly stories about a scared child.

How much did she like Dylan? Ruth didn't know. He looked less like a policeman since he'd shaved off his moustache, but not a lot less. He wasn't her usual type at all. She didn't know his interests or his home circumstances, only that he had kids and was divorced. He seemed caring, which was the most important thing. Even so, she resolved not to mention her father's heart attack, though it was constantly playing on her mind. She wasn't after a heavy relationship, only light relief in a lousy time.

What to wear? Ruth settled for a slightly translucent green top, with a black bra beneath and a long brown skirt. Would she be warm enough? Who cared? She dabbed on eyeliner, smeared on lipstick, put some concealer over a spot on her nose, then went down to meet him. Chris was sitting at the big old dining table. He pushed a gin and tonic in her direction and smiled.

"You look great."

"You're not so bad yourself."

He was wearing a long-sleeved John Smedley Polo top, with moleskin jeans and Timberland boots. His maintenance payments must leave him with enough for luxuries.

"I managed to get us a table at the Lace Market Grill Room," Chris said, "but not until nine-thirty. I hope that's all right."

"Fine."

The Grill Room was a pretty expensive place. Ruth was impressed.

"Anyway, what held you up?" Chris asked, as she sipped her drink.

Ruth told him about meeting Charlotte Jackson. Then she told him her theory about Charlotte and her mother having kidnapped Tom, elaborating slightly on what she'd worked out in the bath. When she'd finished, Chris laughed.

"How many drinks have you had?" he asked, and, for a moment, she felt foolish. Then he went on, "Actually, that's clever. Are you auditioning for a permanent posting with CID, or pitching a plot for a TV film?"

"You tell me," she said.

Chris stroked his chin, thinking. "If – and it's a very big *if* – Louise did do it, she'd want to visit the boy, wherever he is, make sure he's all right. We saw her diary – it's all twelve-hour days and six-day weeks. So, if she was going to see him, Sunday's the day."

"So what do we do?" Ruth asked.

"I'll think about it," Chris said, sceptically. "See

if it makes sense in the morning. But we've talked enough about work. Let's go out and enjoy ourselves."

"I'm really worried about Curt," Julie told Ben.

For once, she'd got a babysitter, and was round at his flat in Mapperley Park.

"Hasn't he phoned?"

"Not for two days. He was staying at a house in the Meadows. I couldn't get the address out of him. I got the phone number using Callback, but he's not there."

"He's probably not answering the phone."

Ben didn't really want to be involved in Curt's living arrangements, which were probably illegal. Part of him wished that the boy would go into a children's home. It would make his and Julie's life a lot easier. Another part of him knew what those homes were like and would wish them on nobody.

"Or he might have gone to Natalie's," Julie said.

"I can't see Maxine hiding him."

Maxine Loscoe, Natalie's mum, was not one of the world's more generous women.

"Would you mind if we went up there, took a look?"

"Can't we just phone?"

"You can't tell if somebody's lying on the phone," Julie said. "And I'd like to talk to Natalie about Curt. He needs her too."

Ben wasn't sure quite how much responsibility a fourteen-year-old girl could be expected to take in the case of a homeless boyfriend. Julie was only seventeen, however, and might see things differently. Sometimes it seemed to Ben that, however old you are, you think you know everything. Only later do you find out how little you were really aware of. One day, would he look back on this relationship as a few months' madness? He didn't want to know the answer.

"All right," he said. "Before we go out to dinner, we'll go and see Natalie."

Singing Candi Staton in the shower, Neil wished that he hadn't been talked into the party. Dancing he didn't mind, if there was decent music, but there rarely was. Conversation was all right, too, up to a point. He'd learned that it was best to lie about what he did: pretend to be a mature student or some kind of technician. He also had to ignore the joints being passed around, the kids off their head on Ecstasy or worse. He was three years older than the average student he met. It felt more like thirty.

When he came downstairs in his dressing gown, Melanie was coming in from the chippy.

"What the hell happened?" she asked.

"Sorry," Neil said, "I'm not with you."

"There's half a packet of white flour all over the front door."

Neil swore. "Kids!" he said. "Some came trick or treating as I was going up for my shower. I couldn't be bothered to answer it."

"Well done," Melanie said, getting out plates for their food. "Just as long as you don't expect me to clear it up."

As Neil sat down to eat, the phone began to ring.

"Don't answer it," Melanie said. "Whatever it is, you haven't time."

She was right, but, after his earlier telling off, Neil took a perverse satisfaction in ignoring her. DI Greasby was on the end of the line. He apologized for calling on Neil. Dylan was unobtainable and the night crime officer was dealing with all kinds of Hallowe'en capers.

"We've just had a call," he said. "Man you saw this afternoon, Wallace…"

Neil couldn't quite read the Inspector's tone. It was obviously serious. Wallace had either abused another kid or killed himself. He hoped it was the latter.

"What's happened?" he asked.

"He's been attacked. On his way to the Queen's Medical Centre now."

"How bad?" Neil asked.

"Put it this way: he won't be abusing any more kids, ever."

13

The night was mild, so they decided to walk into the city, stopping at Natalie's place on the way.

"Where are we going to eat?" Julie asked.

It was the first time that Ben had taken her out for a meal.

"A place called The Lace Market Grill."

"Sounds posh. Sure you can afford it?"

Julie would like to pay her whack in this relationship, but it wasn't likely to happen for a long while.

"They're doing a special discount for police."

"Perk of the job, eh?"

Ben frowned. He didn't like her to suggest that he was anything other than squeaky clean.

"What time are we eating?" she wanted to know.

"Nine. Is that all right?"

"Fine." Jyoti, who was babysitting, didn't mind staying until midnight.

"Is this where they live?"

"Yeah."

Julie had never been to Maxine and Natalie's place before. It was a first-floor apartment in an old house at the cheap end of Mapperley Park, where the area began to merge with the city and St Ann's. There was a light on inside. Ben climbed the stairs but Julie called him back. "Wait for me out of sight, would you? I don't want you scaring Maxine off from opening the door."

Ben had called here before, in an official capacity, when Maxine's husband, Gordon, escaped from the local prison. No one had heard from him since. Julie suspected that he was abroad, with her mum and her Uncle Eddie. The three of them went back a long way.

Julie rang the doorbell. No reply. She rang it again, for longer this time. After a pause, a side window opened.

"We've no sweets!"

"I'm not after sweets," Julie called. "I'm here about Curt, Natalie."

The window closed and Natalie came to the door. She was wearing a threadbare sweater which Julie recognized: one of her brother's.

"You've not got your boyfriend with you. Good."

Julie thought it best not mention that Ben was outside. Natalie was barely fourteen, but streetwise. Most people, seeing her and Curt together, would assume that their ages were reversed.

"Is he here?"

Natalie nodded. "Just for the night. My mum's away, back tomorrow. Julie, what are we going to do with him?"

"I don't know."

"He's talking about us running off somewhere, getting a squat. But I don't want to be homeless."

"They'd pick you up anyhow."

"Maybe, maybe not," Natalie said, with a confidence which Julie probably had at that age. Just let her wait till she got cold, or pregnant, or worse...

"Julie?"

Curt appeared in the hallway, wearing a towelling dressing gown which was way too big for him. It must be Gordon's. Julie grinned, relieved to see him. They didn't go in for hugging or kissing or any of that stuff, but stood awkwardly, each waiting for the other to say something.

"What are we going to do with you?" Julie said, echoing what Natalie had asked her a minute ago.

"I wondered if you'd heard from Mum and Eddie," Curt said, hurriedly. "I was thinking that maybe I could hitch over to France, find them, then Nat could join me. You and Tammy too if—"

134

"I don't know where they are," Julie said. "We've had one poxy postcard from Paris. They're gone, Curt. They don't want us tying them down. We're on our own."

Curt hung his head and Julie cursed herself. Why did she always have to be so blunt?

"Where are you going to stay tomorrow?" she asked.

"I'll find somewhere."

"My mum might not be back till Monday," Natalie said. "You can never tell with her."

"Listen," Julie said. "Come home. What's the worst that can happen? Social Services come and drag you away, put you in care. Next day, you clear off, come back to me. Repeat a few times and they'll soon get tired of it, leave you alone."

"I don't want to go in a home," Curt said. "I don't want people knowing—"

"Oh, sod that!" Julie told him. "Do you really think you've got some kind of reputation to lose? I'll tell you what, though. Don't use this as an excuse to get yourself arrested again, 'cos that'd be really clever. If you get done again, they'll put you away until you're eighteen. And there'll be nothing waiting for you when you get out – not me, not Natalie, nothing."

She could see it in his guilty sideways glance: either he'd been up to something, or he was about to be.

"Think on, Curt," she said. "I've got to go."

Natalie saw her to the door. "Thanks," she said.

"If your mum comes back tomorrow, send him to me," Julie told her. "We'll sort something out."

"I don't think he believes that," Natalie said. "I think he wants to look after himself."

"You and me," Julie replied, "we're all he's got. If he doesn't let us look after him, he's a fool."

Natalie didn't reply. Julie left. Ben was at the bottom of the stairs, rubbing his hands together for warmth, waiting.

"Well?" he said. "Was he there?"

Julie thought for a moment. She could use his advice, but didn't dare draw him in.

"You don't want to know," she said. "Come on, let's go eat."

Alan Wallace was already being operated on when Neil got to the Queen's Medical Centre. It took him ten minutes to find a doctor who could tell him what the situation was.

"He took a severe beating, lost a lot of blood. Tell me, was there an earlier assault?"

"This morning, yes. I don't know if he saw a doctor then."

"What are we talking about here? Jealous husband? The injuries to the groin area are the most severe…"

"I doubt that it's a jealous husband," Neil said, "but a lot of people have got it in for him."

Should he tell this woman what he knew about Wallace? Chances were the news would spread quickly whatever he said. But the police had a duty to protect the paedophile and find whoever had done this to him.

"When do you think he'll be able to tell us what happened?"

"Tomorrow lunchtime at the earliest," the doctor said. "He'll be in a great deal of pain when he does wake up."

"I'll be back," Neil said. "In the meantime, can you make sure nobody leaks this to the media?"

"I'll try," the doctor told him, "but an attack like this is newsworthy."

"I know," Neil said, "but it's too late for the Sundays already. We need the chance to interview the victim and get a head start on the investigation before the media begin a feeding frenzy."

"I understand," the doctor said. "But you'd better tell me – what's he done? A rapist?"

"As bad as," Neil said. "Some would say worse."

The doctor nodded as though she understood. "Whatever he did," she said, "he'll never be able to do it again. They made sure of that."

"*They?*" Neil asked.

"Oh yes, there were at least two of them: a sharp knife and a blunt one, that's what the surgeon said."

Her bleep went off. "You'll have to excuse me."

Neil rang DI Greasby, passed on the news, then

headed home. He'd told Melanie not to wait – she could meet some mates, go to the party without him if she liked. His fish and chips would be ruined, so he'd pick up a pizza instead.

He was going to get his quiet night in after all. Unless, that was, he couldn't resist the investigation and headed over to Villiers House, where Greasby and a couple of beat coppers were carrying out interviews. Trouble was, Wallace had got exactly what was coming to him. Neil rather hoped that whoever did it got away with it.

He pulled up outside a Pizza Parlour on Hucknall Road. As he queued for his Four Seasons a scary thought struck him. What if Wallace had been lying about the mysterious boy alibi? What if he had taken Tom Jackson and the boy was hidden somewhere? In that case, whoever assaulted Alan Wallace had not only taken away his manhood, they had also condemned Tom Jackson to death.

Ruth plumped for goat's cheese tarts with a sundried tomato sauce. Dylan asked for the mixed *hors d'oeuvre* and ordered a bottle of Sauvignon Blanc. Both decided on the sea bream for the main course. Ruth had never had it before. Dylan confessed that he hadn't, either.

"We used to go to Whitby for our holidays, every August without fail. They have all the fish you'd ever want there. But it was always cod and chips.

No, tell a lie, I took the wife one time. We went to the Magpie cafe and splashed out. She had skate and I had monkfish. Quite nice, too, mine was. I ended up finishing half of hers, too. Not a woman of sophisticated tastes, Janice."

"Is that why you broke up?" Ruth asked. Since he'd brought up his ex-wife, she thought she ought to show some interest.

"No, it was the usual thing. The job kept me away all hours and we started growing apart. Faults on both sides. I think we're both over it now. She's got someone else. We put on a good face for the kids."

"That's important."

"Mustn't make them the victims of my cock-ups," Dylan said, then stopped to taste the wine, nodded approval and watched as the waiter poured them a glass each. "Anyway," he continued, "that's enough about my love life."

"You've told me nothing!" Ruth protested, with a grin.

"Met her when I was eighteen, married her at twenty, divorced at thirty. Not a lot else to tell. So now it's your turn. How did a girl from Halifax end up living in Forest Fields?"

Ruth gave him an edited version of her early life, missing out her parents as much as possible.

"I was a late developer where blokes were concerned," she said. "Didn't have my first serious boyfriend until I joined the police."

"What?" Chris said, surprised. "You mean Ben Shipman?"

"No, I was in the police in Halifax, but as a civilian. After school, I trained to be a radio operator."

Ruth ran through the story as they lingered over their starters. At eighteen, when she got the job with the police, she'd left home and moved in with a friend, Cath. They had a two-bedroom flat above an Oxfam shop. People said that the pair of them were like sisters. In some ways, Ruth's friendship with Cath was like her relationship with Clare. Ruth was the plain one, Cath the pretty one, though this wasn't how she put it to Dylan. There were always plenty of blokes after them.

But then Cath went off to university. She'd taken a year's break, found the world of work limiting, and cleared off to Newcastle. Ruth didn't have the grades to get on a good course, didn't want to go into debt to finance a degree which she wasn't sure she wanted to do anyway. She and Cath kept in touch, but Newcastle was a long way from Halifax and, inevitably, they saw less of each other.

After that, Ruth's first real boyfriend lived with her for a while. Pete was twenty-two, a carpet fitter. They'd been going out for three months, after he chatted up Cath one night and ended up with Ruth instead. It was a casual thing. Soon they got on each other's nerves, him expecting her to do everything to subsidize his drinking and eating. In the end, it was cheaper, easier, to live alone, so she asked him to leave. That was her only long-term relationship before Ben Shipman.

"So, you see, there isn't a lot to tell about my love life, either."

"I get the feeling that you're leaving plenty out," Chris said, finishing his food, which he'd devoured greedily.

"Don't come the detective with me," Ruth warned, playfully.

"Right you are. Will you excuse me a minute?"

While Chris went to the loo, Ruth thought about that time, before she became a police officer. It wasn't the happiest part of her life. During the year and a half she lived above the shop, she'd gone home occasionally: Sunday dinners, relatives' visits, that kind of thing. But it was always a strain. Dad was over-friendly, Mum more distant than before. She'd had a nervous breakdown when Ruth was just a kid and still took antidepressants from time to time. Ruth was scared that she was heading that way again. Other times, she feared that depressive illness had been passed on to her – that, in time, she too was bound to break down.

In the end, she'd decided to leave Halifax. At first, she thought about a transfer. There were jobs going all over. Newcastle appealed for a while, but she knew that the friendship with Cath would never be the same. In the end, she chose Nottingham not for what it was, but for what it wasn't: not too far away; not in the North, but decidedly not in the South; not too expensive; the police force not bad, but not too hard to get into, either.

Quite when she decided to become a police officer rather than a radio operator, Ruth never knew. It just happened. In the interview, she said that she'd got to know the job, and it appealed to her. She'd wanted a job which absorbed her, which took her out of herself. Ruth knew the job had a down side. She thought she knew all about the paperwork, the empty hours, the institutional sexism, but she knew she could handle it – thought she knew.

She enjoyed the training. In Clare, she made the closest friend she'd ever had. They got placed on shifts in adjoining areas. Soon, though, the job began to disappoint her. Clare seemed happier where she was, at least until her boyfriend died, so Ruth moved. But transferring from South to East hadn't made it any easier, not with having to work alongside Ben. Ruth was flattered by Chris Dylan's interest in her, though. You never knew. Maybe things were about to change for the good.

She finished her glass of wine and decided that it was best to wait for Dylan before helping herself to another one. Then her mind went blank for a moment, waking up the worry which had been burrowed there all day. She wondered how her father was.

14

"Any witnesses?" Neil asked the DI when he'd
brought him up to date on Wallace's condition. In the end, he'd been unable to resist going
to Villiers House. Easier to report in person than to
ring with the details.

"Nothing concrete," Greasby replied. "We've
been round all the residents who're in. They say
there were a few trick or treaters round earlier – last
lot about six-thirty, which is half an hour to an hour
before the attack took place."

"Who found him?"

"Nobody. He managed to crawl to a phone. Take
a look if you like. It's not a pretty sight."

Neil stuck his head round the yellow tape which
Scene of Crime had used to seal off the area. There

was a heavy trail of blood leading from the kitchen to the phone, which was above the telly.

"Are the sweets gone?" he asked.

"Hmm?" Greasby queried, distracted by something going on on the floor below.

"He had a boxful of sweets to give out to kids – mini Mars bars, that kind of thing."

"Still there," Greasby said, then swore. A woman in a smart mac was climbing the stairs, followed by a burly bloke with a video camera.

"Detective Inspector Greasby? I'm Helen Chase, from Central News."

"No comment," Greasby said.

"I haven't asked you any questions yet!" Chase protested.

"Makes no odds, I'll still have no comment. And this is a crime scene. You can't come any closer."

"Wait," the reporter said. "I have something to trade. We got an anonymous tip-off earlier. We were told that what happened here was connected with the Tom Jackson kidnapping case."

"Who says that Tom Jackson was kidnapped?" Greasby asked. "Nobody knows. You don't. I don't."

He turned to Neil. "Take a statement from her about this anonymous call. Don't confirm or deny anything about Wallace."

"Sir."

Neil joined Helen Chase in the foyer. "About this

call," he said, after making sure that he wasn't being filmed.

"Man. Not much accent, according to the switchboard operator. Middle class, maybe. All he said was what I intimated to your Inspector – that Wallace was in hospital and he had it coming to him for kidnapping Tom Jackson. Is that right? Did he take the boy?"

"I've got nothing to tell you about that," Neil said. "Was the call tape recorded?"

"No. We don't do that. Do you have any idea where Tom Jackson is?"

"No," Neil said. "Did the caller give any reason for believing that Wallace had taken Tom Jackson?"

"No," Helen said. "My turn. Why was Wallace placed in a hostel opposite a nursery school?"

"Nothing to do with us," Neil said. "What else do you know?"

"The caller described Wallace's injuries," she told him.

"In what terms?"

"How to put this?" Chase said, with a slightly facetious smile. "He implied that Mr Wallace no longer has the full meat and two veg."

"Let's just say it was a particularly nasty attack."

"But a singularly appropriate one? Almost biblical?"

"Old Testament," Neil told her, then realized that he'd said too much. "Look, if you're going to report this, don't bring Tom Jackson into it. The parents are upset enough already. It wouldn't be productive."

"But what if Wallace has the toddler tied up, concealed somewhere?"

It was a fair point, and one which had already occurred to Neil. He hadn't had the chance to track down Wallace's alibi yet. His gut feeling, however, was that the man had been telling him the truth. He had nothing to do with the disappearance.

"Off the record," he told the reporter.

"All right."

"It's unlikely. Not impossible, but unlikely."

"Somebody believes it," Chase challenged.

"Or wants us to," Neil said.

"What are you implying?"

"Nothing," Neil told her. "Just thinking aloud."

The meal was good, but the conversation had become desultory. Ruth had little in common with Chris apart from the job, which they avoided discussing. She'd been toying with the idea of spending the night with him. It would take her mind off things. But there was, she decided, no such thing as casual sex. Better to keep things friendly but professional. He'd understand.

Then something happened which changed her mind. Coming back from the Ladies, she saw a couple in the corner. It was a poor table, near the door. The man had his back to Ruth and his head bent conspiratorially. The girl looked like a model. Waiters gave her discreet glances when they walked by. Maybe she wasn't conventionally beautiful, but she had something special about her, something sexy. And her eyes glowed like those of a woman in love.

Ruth wouldn't normally have recognized her, but she was struck by the way her bloke nodded his head. It was Ben. And the woman, she saw now, was the same one she'd seen in a dressing gown one early morning three weeks before: his new girl-friend, Julie Wilder. What was he doing taking her to a restaurant like this when Ruth had been lucky if he took her to a cheap Italian joint?

"Coffee?" Chris offered.

"No. Let's just go."

He gave her an enquiring look and she added, "We can have a drink at my place, if you like."

"I like."

Chris got the bill with professional speed, refused Ruth's offer to go dutch, and dumped cash on the table. As they headed to the door, he put a tentative arm around her waist. Ruth reciprocated immediately. They walked past Ben and Julie's table entwined like the lovers they were about to become.

Chris had a taxi waiting outside.

"Do you do this sort of thing often?" Ruth asked.

"Not often enough. Look, I've got a bottle of

bubbly at home, if you're interested."

"I'm interested."

He told the cab driver where to go, then they kissed. *This is a mistake,* Ruth told herself. But she had plenty of booze inside her. It was easiest to let his hands go where they wanted, to head for the empty oblivion of drunken desire.

CID and SOCO knocked off at half eleven, when most punters would be back from the pub. Neil was the last to leave. Melanie would be at the party. He had nothing to hurry home for.

"What's going on?"

It was the bloke from earlier, the one whose kids died in a fire.

"There was an assault in room five."

"That Wallace bloke?"

"Yes. Between seven and half-past. I don't suppose you saw anything?"

The man thought for a moment. "No. Well, not in here, but…"

"Go on," Neil said.

"I was on my way over to my sister's in Mapperley. Let's see, the bus goes at 7:18, and I was only just in time, so it would have been about quarter past. There was – it's probably got nothing to do with it."

"Go on, please," Neil said.

"This kid was outside, twelve or thirteen, wearing a

luminous ghoul mask – like a member of the Addams Family, the one who looks like Frankenstein's monster – and there were two men with him."

"Men?"

"Tall, darkly dressed. I didn't get a good look at them. I was in a hurry. But the odd thing was, they seemed to be telling him what to do. I only caught a few words. *Make sure you leave the door open*, it sounded like. I assumed they were telling him to be safe when he went knocking on doors, but there was something funny about them."

"Like what?" Neil asked. "If you can think of anything at all..."

"I'm not sure."

"Can you describe their faces?"

"No. I didn't see them. Oh, but they were both wearing woolly hats."

"Bobble hats?"

He thought for a moment. "No. No bobble. But they were kind of bunched up. Like—"

"Like a balaclava which had been pushed up, perhaps?"

"Yes, that's it, precisely. Dark coloured bala-clavas, rolled up."

"You've been a lot of help," Neil said. "I'll probably come by tomorrow, take a formal state-ment, if that's all right."

"I'm not going anywhere."

One thing was clear, Neil thought, as he drove

home. Alan Wallace was set up. But who by? The phone call to Central suggested that this was related to Tom Jackson's disappearance. Vigilantes? It didn't ring true. Unless someone knew what Wallace had done to Tom Jackson and, rather than go to the police, had taken the law into their own hands. Yes, that was a possibility.

Neil needed to know the truth about Alan Wallace's alibi. He'd get on to someone from the local school tomorrow, find out how many Curts they had, aged between fourteen and sixteen. If Wallace's alibi checked out, it might be better to look elsewhere for his assailant. Meanwhile, a two-year-old boy was still missing. For him, time was running out.

15

Ben slept badly, haunted, unexpectedly, by the sight of Ruth with Chris Dylan at the restaurant the night before. He'd thought that she would take longer than that to get over him. And to go out with a letch like Dylan! The only good thing to be said about the DS was that he was no longer cheating on his wife: she'd dumped him. Ruth deserved better. At least she hadn't noticed Ben and Julie, who'd been having a brilliant night. Nor had Julie seen Ruth.

His girlfriend slept beside him, with Tammy gurgling happily in the bed between them. It was gone eleven. Ben got up to make tea. While the kettle was heating up, he dialled his home phone number, punching in the code which allowed him to retrieve his messages from the machine. There was just one, from Neil Foster.

"I need your help, mate. There was a GBH last night on Alan Wallace. I'm trying to work out if it was connected with the Tom Jackson business. I know this sounds strange, but Wallace's alibi for when the boy went missing is that he was with Curt Wilder – at least, it's probably Curt. There's nobody else called Curt at his school, so ... sorry, I'm rambling. Didn't get much sleep last night. Thing is, I know Curt's hiding, but you can probably find him. If you could arrange for me to have a word ... page me. Cheers."

Great! Ben thought. Curt in yet more murky waters. He could call Neil now, tell him where Curt was before the boy cleared off again. But if Curt saw a police officer at the door, he'd do a runner anyway. So Ben would have to get Julie to broker a meeting.

The kettle boiled. Ben put tea bags into mugs, annoyed as usual that Julie didn't have a teapot. He liked it to brew properly. What was Curt doing with Alan Wallace anyway? It didn't bear thinking about. He went upstairs to wake his girlfriend.

"What time is it?" Ruth asked Chris, who had brought her breakfast in bed.

"Just gone eleven."

"The beginning of three blissful days off," Ruth told him. She meant to get away as quickly as possible.

153

"I've been thinking about what you said last night," Chris said, suddenly. "You know, it could be a good idea to do some discreet surveillance."

"Oh, right." She hadn't realized that he'd taken her seriously.

"Your hunch, not mine," Chris said. "I'd be just as happy – no, make that *happier* – if we stayed in bed all day."

Ruth wasn't feeling remotely randy. "Tempting," she said, making up her mind. "But I think we should follow Louise Jackson all the same. Have you got any aspirin, paracetamol? My head feels like a breaker's yard."

He brought her two Solpadeine, then put on Radio Trent. The news was coming to an end.

"Police are investigating a vicious attack on a man living in a Nottingham hostel. Alan Wallace, forty-four, is recovering in hospital after men with knives broke into his room early yesterday evening. It is believed that they may have used a child in a Hallowe'en mask as a decoy."

The report was carefully worded so that, unless you knew who Alan Wallace was, you wouldn't guess that he was a paedophile. If you did, the motive for the attack was easy to work out.

"Did you hear that?" Ruth asked Chris.

"Yeah. Poor sod. Local hysteria because of Tom

Jackson, I'll bet."

"Wallace is no innocent," Ruth said.

"Who is? I don't mind a bloke getting beaten up for something he's done but we can't do him for, but Wallace no more snatched that kid than I did. Now, get a move on with those croissants. We want to get to Louise Jackson's before she goes out for the day."

"Better check if she's there," Ruth said, and picked up Dylan's phone.

Louise Jackson lived in The Park. She was ex-directory, but had given Ruth her number. She dialled 141 first, so that Louise couldn't use Callback to find out who she was. The phone rang several times.

"Yes?" There was water running in the background.

"I'm sorry to disturb you, madam," Ruth said, making her Yorkshire accent as broad as she could. "I'm from Duffield Double Glazing and we have a representative in your area this week—"

"I'm just getting in the bath and I'm not interested. This phone's ex-directory. Where did you get the number?"

"Sorry to disturb you," Ruth said again, and hung up.

She sipped her coffee and smiled at Dylan. "I think I've got time to have a shower before we go out. Have you got a towel I can use?"

She finished her breakfast and, when he returned

with the towel, covered herself. In the bathroom there were rubber ducks and bubble bath shaped like a space ship. It was weird, being with a bloke who had kids. The water turned hot quickly, almost scalding her, but Ruth didn't turn it down.

Neil's pager vibrated as he left the Queen's Medical Centre. He read the message: Ben, on a number he didn't recognize. When he called, Ben was brief.

"I know where he is, but he won't be there for long. I think it's best if we just show up at the place. Julie can go in, talk him into talking to you. All right?"

"Fine," Neil said. "I appreciate this. Shall I come and pick you up?"

"You're in your own car, yeah?"

"Yeah."

"OK. I'm at—"

"It's all right," Neil said. "I know where it is."

As he drove to the Maynard Estate, Neil thought about Alan Wallace, who had regained consciousness briefly and been able to answer a few questions. Wallace admitted inviting a boy into his room yesterday evening. The lad had only been inside a moment when the door burst open, and two masked men charged in. They had knocked the paedophile unconscious almost immediately, which was a mercy for Wallace, given what came next. The shock might have killed him.

Nobody had heard the cold-blooded attack. When Wallace came to, in agony, he managed to crawl to the phone and dial three nines before passing out again. His description of the attackers was less than useless. He hadn't seen the boy decoy's face, couldn't even remember the colour of his hair behind the mask. Without a confession, even if the police found his assailants, it would be very hard to prove their identity.

Ben got into the front of the car, Julie and her baby into the back. Julie gave Neil the briefest of "hello"s. She was very pretty, he saw in the rear view mirror, but too young for Ben. She looked like a sixth former. But Melanie was still only nineteen, and what was a year or two? He wondered how his girlfriend had got on at the party the night before. She hadn't called this morning and he hadn't liked to phone her. She was probably sleeping late.

"Good night last night?" Neil asked Ben, when Julie had gone into the Loscoes' apartment alone, leaving Ben holding the baby.

"Pretty good, yeah. Went to the Lace Market Grill."

"Smart."

"Yeah," Ben said, ruminatively. "Ruth was there, with Dylan."

"Really?"

Neil had noticed Chris putting the moves on Ruth. It was a standing joke in CID: the sergeant would have a go at anything in a skirt, but stayed away from married women and those with boyfriends in the job. Chris specialized in pulling women when they were on the rebound. He'd even had a go at Clare, shortly after she and Neil split up. His relationships rarely lasted more than a week. Neil didn't say any of this to Ben, who probably had a good idea what the DS was like anyway.

"She can do better than him," was all Ben said next.

Julie came out before they could discuss it further. "He'll see you," she said.

The four of them went into the apartment, a shabby set of rented rooms. Natalie was still in her dressing gown. What kind of mother left a girl her age on her own overnight? Neil wondered.

"Curt's in the bedroom. Julie said you wanted a quiet word with him."

"That's right," Neil said. Curt might be embarrassed to discuss Wallace in front of his girlfriend.

It was Natalie's room. There were furry animals, posters of boy bands on the wall. Curt sat on the single bed, wearing torn jeans and a T-shirt which was too small for him – probably one of Natalie's, given that it had a picture of Garfield on the front. At least there were no track marks on his arms. Neil had come across junkies younger than him.

"What can I do for you?" the boy asked.

Neil got straight to the point. "There's this guy —
he's a suspect in a case, and he gave you as his alibi."

"Me? I haven't agreed to alibi anyone!" Curt
protested.

That was a typical criminal's response. It didn't
occur to him that Neil might be asking for a genuine
alibi.

"Thing is, he didn't know at the time that he
needed an alibi. The way he describes it, you were
put in a bit of an embarrassing situation…"

"Like…?"

Curt's eyes narrowed. The puzzlement on his
face brought out the resemblance to his sister, which
was only slight. Neil decided to go for the formal
approach.

"Can you tell me where you were between one
and one-thirty last Wednesday afternoon?"

"Yeah. I was skiving off school."

"Where?"

Curt thought for a moment. "This big old house.
I was meeting someone there."

"Name of…?"

"That doesn't matter," Curt said. "I was wet.
Some old bloke invited me up to his room to dry off,
get a drink. So I went."

"What time was that?"

"I left school after registration. That's about ten
to one. So this'd be ten past, at the latest."

"And how long were you with this man?"

"Twenty minutes, tops."

It was enough. Neil pulled a photo out of his wallet. "Is this him?"

Curt glanced at him. "Yeah. Alan something. I know who he is now. Heard people talking about him. Saw some blokes push him in the river. I knew what he was before that, though."

"He tried it on?" Neil asked, keeping his voice casual.

"Yeah."

"According to him, he offered you money."

"I think he shouted something after I turned him down. But I didn't stay to find out what he was offering, just did a runner."

"You did the right thing," Neil said. "Good. That's all. You've been very helpful. Thanks."

"Does this mean that Wallace couldn't have taken that kid?"

"It does."

"Poor little sod's had it, hasn't he?" Curt said, compassion in his voice.

"Yes," Neil said. "It looks like he has." He got up to go.

"You didn't see me here today," Curt warned.

"As far as anybody looking for you is concerned," Neil said, "I didn't see you at all. I just needed to clear that up."

He left the youth and joined the others in the kitchen. "All done," he said.

"You go," Ben told him. "We can walk home from here."

"Whatever you say. Thanks for helping."

"Any time."

Ben looked completely out of place, Neil thought, as he drove to the station. But no more than Neil himself would have done at that student party the night before. Maybe they were both barking up the wrong tree.

He changed his mind and, instead of going to the station, went to Melanie's. She didn't answer the doorbell. He had a key, could have gone in to wait for her, but didn't. For a minute, he thought about going to see Clare. She could probably do with some company. But she was back living with her mother and it felt weird. So he drove to work, where he would do more unpaid overtime.

Louise Jackson left her house at twelve-twenty, driving her Lexus on to the Derby Road towards the old university. Chris and Ruth followed. They seemed to be back on a professional basis now, Ruth having got him to stop at her house so that she could change into some sensible clothes. She'd made herself deliberately dowdy, a policewoman at work. That was how she wanted Chris to see her.

At the big roundabout by the university, Louise turned right, heading into Wollaton. She took another right turn and Chris had trouble keeping up. These streets were full of odd turnings and cul-de-sacs. But they found her, parked outside a suburban semi. Chris pulled up at the far end of the road.

"Shall I get out?" Ruth suggested. "Take a look?"

"Wait," Chris said. "I think she's still in the car. She hasn't had time to go anywhere yet."

At this distance, it was impossible to see through the shaded windows of Louise's car, so they waited. If she had gone into a house, it could be one of four or five. They watched all of them. Five minutes passed. Ten.

"She must have gone inside one of the houses," Ruth said.

"But what if she hasn't? Or what if she comes out while you're having a nosy and recognizes you? We're all right here," Dylan insisted. "What-ho?"

A girl in a blue anorak was coming out of one of the houses: Charlotte Jackson. She got into the passenger seat of the Lexus, which started up immediately.

"Picking up the daughter," Ruth said.

"But from where?" Dylan asked. "Head down."

They both ducked as the Lexus, which had turned round, came out of the road. Then Dylan started the engine, drove down the road and did a similar five-point turn. The house which Charlotte had been in was number eight, a standard three-bedroomed, former council house. It had net curtains, but so did nearly every other house on the street.

"Aren't we going to follow her?" Ruth asked.

"She'll be going home, I should think," Dylan said, "but we might as well confirm it."

"What next?" Ruth asked, when they were on the Derby Road. "Get a search warrant?"

"That'd be jumping the gun," Chris said. "The girl was probably only visiting a friend. We'll check the electoral register, find out who lives at number eight. If it turns out to be officially empty, that's when we get a search warrant."

"Still," Ruth said, "definitely some kind of a result."

"A result," Chris agreed. "Fancy some lunch?"

"No," she said. "You'd better drop me at home. I've got some family stuff to sort. But call me later if you do get a search warrant, please. I'd like to be there."

"You're the boss," Dylan said.

The Tom Jackson case being at a dead end, DI Greasby had decided to double up the Incident Room to deal with the Alan Wallace attack as well. Neil was going through the papers which had been prepared for court before the charges were dropped. Greasby was on the phone to a neighbouring force. He was trying to get Lincoln CID to establish discreetly whether Malcolm Green, the father of the two children assaulted by Wallace, had an alibi for the night before. The Greens had moved to Lincoln not long after the assault.

"They've been put through hell already," he was saying, "but it'll be in the papers tomorrow so we need to get to them first, keep them informed and eliminate them from our enquiries. Thanks."

He turned to Neil. "We need to visit the Carter family, on Davies Road. Find out what they were up to last night."

This was the family of the nine-year-old Wallace had abused.

"The son, too?"

"Especially the son. Though he's a bit young to have been the decoy."

"The family would never put him through that."

"Probably not," Greasby agreed. "But with the mask on, Wallace might not have recognized him. We have to look at every angle."

"It doesn't have to have been connected with a kid who Wallace abused," Neil said. He didn't want it to be John Carter or his son.

"You don't think so?" Greasby asked. "The men who mugged Wallace, threw him in the river, sure, they were just have-a-go vigilantes. But this was planned. They knocked him out then mutilated his genitals. Whoever did it had a serious motive."

Neil agreed. "I was talking to the people at the Paedophile Investigation Unit. They reckon that, for every indecent assault that comes to our attention, there are another nine unreported. So, in Wallace's case, there could be a lot of other people with a powerful grudge against him."

"True," Greasby said. "It'd make an interesting interview, wouldn't it? We ask Wallace for the names of kids he *didn't* get caught abusing so that we can check whether their dads attacked him. He's sure to come clean."

"Can you imagine the publicity if it was the Carters?" Neil asked.

"Doesn't bear thinking about," Greasby agreed. "They'd be national heroes. As it is, there'll be copycat attacks if the press get the full story. I've already had the Chief Constable asking me to keep it as low key as possible. You know what he said? *We could really use a break in the Tom Jackson case, take the heat off this story*. As if we haven't done everything we can do... Hello, Chris."

Dylan waved cheerfully as he walked into the Incident Room.

"Glad to see I'm not the only one out on a Sunday," the DS said, with a grin.

"You'd have been with us last night if you'd had your pager switched on," Greasby told him. "Your answering machine was off too. Hot date?"

"Hot enough."

"Anyone we know?"

"Ruth Clarke – probationer who's just transferred to East."

"Pretty girl," Greasby said. "Result?"

"Result."

Greasby smiled, vicariously enjoying Dylan's conquest. Neil felt bad about Ruth being the subject of station banter. But they had more important matters to discuss.

"Shall we head for the Carters, then?" he asked Greasby.

"I guess we'd better. Got anything for us, Chris?"

"Just a sniff of a lead on the missing kid. I'll check it out, let you know."

Ian and Neil drove to West Bridgford in the DI's Rover.

"Nice kid, Ruth Clarke," Ian Greasby told Neil. "Chris could do a lot worse than settle with someone like her."

Neil muttered something which might pass for assent.

"He won't, though," Greasby added, with a tolerant laugh.

16

Sam looked shattered. She was loading dirty clothes straight from her suitcase into the washing machine.

"Good holiday?" Ruth asked.

"Brilliant," Sam said, though her expression remained gloomy.

"You look like you could do with going to bed for forty-eight hours."

"You're probably right," Ruth's landlady admitted. "Actually, I've been waiting for you to get back."

"Bought me some duty-free?"

"Not exactly," Sam said, closing the washer. "I think you ought to sit down." Ruth did as she was told.

"Your mum rang," Sam said. "There were two messages on the machine when I got in."

"I didn't come home last night."

"I gathered. She rang again an hour ago."

"Is he dead?" Ruth asked, matter-of-factly.

"He had a second heart attack. They don't expect him to last the day."

Ruth looked at her watch. Half twelve. She could be there by two.

"I'm sorry to be the bearer of bad news," Sam said.

"It's all right," Ruth told her. "It wasn't unexpected. I'm glad you had a good holiday. Go on, go and get some kip."

Sam came over and tried to hug her, half succeeding. The phone began to ring.

"I'll get it," Ruth said. "It's probably for me."

What would she tell Mum? *I'll come when he's dead?* But it wasn't Mum calling.

"This is Charlotte Jackson." The girl sounded terse, angry.

"Oh … hi."

"Why were you following me and Mum today?"

Ruth was taken aback. Had she and Dylan done such a bad job? Should she deny it?

"Well spotted," she said.

"My mum saw you first. Said she got a funny phone call which made her suspicious. You don't seriously think that she had anything to do with Tom's disappearance, do you?"

"We have to explore every angle," Ruth replied half-heartedly.

"Why don't you believe me?"

You should always believe children, unless there was a compelling reason not to, Ruth knew that.

"I get the feeling there's something you're holding back," Ruth told her. Charlotte said nothing.

"What were you doing in Wollaton?" Ruth asked.

"That's none of your—" Charlotte didn't finish the sentence.

"I'm sorry if we invaded your privacy," Ruth told her. "But your brother's life is at stake, so—"

"Don't tell me what I already know!" Charlotte asserted, angrily.

Ruth kept quiet for a while. One of them had to break the silence, though, and she was the one who was supposed to be grown up.

"Do you want to meet?" she asked. "Talk about it?"

"I guess."

"I don't have much time," Ruth told her. "It would have to be soon."

"Come round now if you like. I'm at Mum's."

"I'll be there in twenty minutes."

Ruth put down the phone. What was she doing? Should she call her own mother, tell her she was on the way? Ruth rushed up to her room, collected some clean underwear and toiletries, keeping her options open. Then she got in her car and drove towards The Park to meet Charlotte Jackson.

The Carter family, unlike the Greens, hadn't moved. Maybe that was because Wallace's offences hadn't happened in the family home.

"They're away," the next-door neighbour told Neil before he could ring the doorbell.

"Do you know where?"

"Couldn't say. Relatives, I think."

"When did they go?"

"Yesterday, some time."

"OK. Thanks. Appreciate it."

Across the street a boy was watching from his bedroom window. When he saw Neil looking at him, the lad – who was thirteen or so – ducked out of sight, not an unusual reaction.

Neil got back into the car. "That's that then," he told Greasby.

"I wouldn't count on it."

Lincoln CID had got back to them. The whole Green family had a cast iron alibi. They'd been at a fireworks party with dozens of other people.

"Since we're passing, sir," Neil said, "perhaps we could pay a courtesy call on the Jacksons, reassure them that we're still…"

"…but we're not, are we?" Greasby said, not letting him finish the sentence. The operation was being scaled down. Major Crimes had moved on to investigating a murder in Sneinton. Tom Jackson was probably dead. Either that or he had been illicitly adopted and was a long way away by now.

"You're right, though," Greasby said. "We should go. Then you can visit the Queen's Med, see if Wallace is awake enough to tell us about any other enemies he might have."

Riverside Estate was quiet. A light drizzle fell on the lawns at the back. There was a light on in 12A. Greasby rang the bell.

"You've got the relationship," he told Neil. "You do the talking."

Tony Jackson came to the door.

"There's no news," Neil said straight away, not wanting to raise hopes or fears. "We're just calling to check how you are, see if anything's come up."

One of the Sunday newspapers had offered a £50,000 reward for information leading to the return of Tom Jackson. They might contact the family direct if something came up.

"Nothing," Tony said. "But come in, please."

Jenny sat in an armchair, staring at the TV, which was showing random Ceefax pages with a sound-track from some Hollywood musical. She didn't look up when Tony turned it off. The woman had aged ten years, Neil saw. Greasby stood awkwardly in the doorway. Neil accepted the chair that Tony Jackson pulled out.

"We haven't given up hope yet," Neil told him.

"Do you ever get the feeling that you're being punished?"

"No," Neil said. "You mustn't think of it like that."

"Oh, but I do. I can't help it."

Neil changed the subject, asked some questions which he already knew the answers to, pretended to take notes. Finally, Jenny spoke.

"That bloke who got attacked last night. Was that anything to do with this?"

"We don't think so," Neil said. "Alan Wallace had a definite alibi for when Tom went missing. I checked it myself."

"I'd hate to think of…" she stopped herself and looked at her husband.

"When something like this happens, you think of everything," Tony said. "Every possible thing that could have been done to him. You understand?"

"Yes," Neil said. He felt desperately sorry for them. If their son wasn't found, he knew, they were likely to split up. This often happened when a child died. It had happened to Clare's parents. It had already happened to Tony Jackson once. What had he done to deserve such disaster happening again? It was a fair enough question.

"I'm sorry," Tony said. "I'm forgetting my manners. Can I get you a drink?"

"No," Neil said. "We're not stopping."

Now Greasby took his turn to speak. "Inevitably," he said, "the search for Tom will get less publicity as the days go by. We don't want you to think we're giving up. If you need any information, any time, Neil's your man. I'm going to give you my home number too."

"Thank you," Tony said. "We appreciate it."

They left with as much haste as they decently could. Two doors down, a cat was scratching an expensive wooden door. A middle-aged man with a paunch let the animal in.

"What did you think?" Neil asked the DI.

"Sad, sad people."

"He seemed like a guilty man," Neil said. Statistics still pointed to a family member being responsible for the boy's disappearance, though none of the evidence did.

"We're all guilty men," Greasby said, dismissively, "but I don't think the father's guilty of this. To be honest, Neil, I'm getting the feeling that this might be one of the ones where we never find out."

They drove back to the station in silence.

"You ought to go," Natalie said. "You can't trust the police. They probably went straight to Social Services. They'll have someone round here any minute."

"On a Sunday?" Curt said. "Nah."

Curt did trust Ben Shipman – up to a point. And

that CID bloke had seemed pretty straight with him.

"Aren't you going to tell me what it was they wanted?"

Curt shrugged. He wasn't going to spill the story about Wallace to Natalie. She might suspect that Curt had encouraged him. Anyhow, the whole thing was far too embarrassing.

"I saw this bloke," he explained vaguely, "at a time when he might have been somewhere else. I'm his alibi, I suppose."

"So it's nothing you've done? They don't know about that house you were squatting in?"

"No," Curt told her. "If it came to it, I could probably go back there tonight."

Though it was risky, returning to a place where you'd nearly been caught. Also, that was the one place where Trev would know to look for him. He didn't know where Natalie lived, thankfully.

"Stay here tonight," Natalie said.

"What if your mum turns up out of the blue?"

"So we have a row," Natalie said, dismissively.

"And I have to find somewhere to go in the middle of the night."

"She wouldn't do that."

"Wouldn't she?" Curt hadn't really tested Maxine Loscoe's temper yet.

"I'll hide you," Nat said. "You can stay in my room. Mum hardly goes in there. I'll sneak you out in the morning before I go to school."

"I guess," Curt said.

They began to move his stuff from the living room to under the bed in Natalie's room. If her mum returned unexpectedly, Curt would join it. There was just about room for him.

"I've had an idea," he said, when they'd finished.

"What?"

"A place I can go where the people are away. Another of the houses that Trev delivers newspapers to. If they're not back tomorrow, it probably means that they'll be gone another week."

"Is it safe?" Natalie asked.

"Fairly. And it's a lot smarter than where I was before."

"Good." Natalie gave him a cuddle. "But you can't keep moving for ever, can you?"

"Why not?" Curt said. "Some people do."

All the same, he knew that she was right. Winter wasn't here yet, and it would go on for weeks and weeks. It was already too cold to spend loads of time on the street. Freedom could be frightening, when you had too much of it. But Curt wasn't going to admit to his girlfriend that he'd rather be at school.

"So, where is it you're going?" Natalie asked him.

To hell, Curt thought, if I'm not more careful.

17

Ruth didn't know why she was here. She could have called Chris, got him to handle the situation. But she'd made some kind of connection with Charlotte the day before. She'd given the girl her number. She couldn't just back off.

Charlotte let Ruth into the smart, modern apartment. She was wearing jeans with a baggy, black Guinness sweatshirt and looked pale but focused, unlike Ruth herself.

"How's your father?" Charlotte asked.

"Worse," Ruth said.

"Then why are you still here?"

"There are … issues," Ruth said, remembering the words from late night phone conversations in lonely callboxes.

"I understand."

The house had the kind of sparse look that Ruth would choose if she had the money and her own place: simple, Swedish-style furniture and pale hardwood floors – an uncluttered look. Louise Jackson came in with a pot of tea on a butler's tray.

"Hello again," she said.

"Hi," Ruth said, timidly. For some reason, she'd expected the mother to be out of the way. Was this to be a personal conversation, or a formal one, where an adult ought to be present?

"You followed me this morning," Louise said.

"Yes. I rang you up, too, pretended to be selling double glazing. Sorry."

"I'm sure you're only doing your job," Louise said.

Ruth didn't confess that she and Chris had been freelancing. "Yes," she said.

"Have you checked out the address that I picked Charlotte up from?"

"No. But my colleague is doing that."

"I see."

Mother and daughter looked at each other. "What do you think?" Louise asked Charlotte.

"I want to tell her," Charlotte replied, quietly.

"Very well. If you're sure."

Ruth turned to Charlotte, who now looked calmer than her mother.

"It's my therapist," she said. "The house. I go once a month for counselling."

"I see," Ruth said.

"No, you don't. I used to go once a week. I'm a lot better now."

"What was ... is the problem?" Ruth asked.

Charlotte looked Ruth straight in the eye and said, calmly, "When I was eight years old, after my brother died, my father had sex with me, several times. When Mum found out, she threw him out. I've been in counselling since then."

"I see." Ruth didn't know what else to say.

"Did you go to the police?" she asked, when Charlotte didn't volunteer anything else.

Charlotte shook her head. "What good would that have done? Dad was messed up. He lost his son and his marriage. I loved him. I let him do what he did to me."

"You are ... were a child," Ruth said. "Consent's not an issue here."

"Afterwards," Charlotte went on, "he would cry, apologize. When Mum found out, he was relieved."

"Tony's been in counselling with Charlotte and me," Louise told Ruth. "We've resolved a lot of things."

"You've forgiven him?" Ruth asked.

"In a way," Louise said, her expression cold, weary. "We couldn't save the marriage, but I didn't want Charlotte to lose a father as well as a brother. Tom's disappearance has hit her very hard, bringing it all back."

"Yes," Ruth said. "I can imagine."

"That's all," Charlotte told her. "Now you know."

"Does his new wife know?" Ruth asked.

"I haven't asked him," Louise said.

Ruth looked at Charlotte. "I don't think so," the girl answered.

"Do you think she'd have married him if she did?"

Charlotte said nothing.

"We don't want this to go any further," Louise said.

"I don't know if I can agree to that," Ruth told her. "Who knows already?"

"There was a social worker involved before we found the therapist."

"No police?" Ruth asked.

"No," Charlotte said. "I wouldn't have pressed charges, so the social worker said it wasn't necessary."

"Maybe not," Ruth said. "Most things like this don't end up in court. But now you've told me, I have to inform my superiors."

"Don't," Charlotte pleaded.

"Sorry," Ruth said. "I don't have any choice in the matter."

"I warned you that she'd have to," Louise said quietly to her daughter. She must have known what would happen. Maybe she even wanted to punish her ex. Ruth wouldn't blame her.

"What good will it do?" Charlotte asked.

Ruth thought for a moment. She really had no choice in a situation like this. Her training had drummed that into her. At the time, she'd wished she'd known the ins and outs earlier.

"An officer will interview your dad, put your … allegations to him. He won't have to reply to them, but at least they'll be on record. Later, if custody becomes an issue or the question of charges against him on this or a similar matter occurs, there'll be a record."

"You're covering yourself," Louise said. "That's what it boils down to."

"Yes," Ruth said. "We have to. This is probably the most sensitive area we deal with."

"My dad's been through hell these last few days," Charlotte said, her voice rising. Ruth could feel the girl turning against her. It was understandable. But this was her job.

"Whoever interviews him will choose the time carefully and do it in a sensitive way," she said. "I don't suppose that Jenny will be told. But he did wrong. He needs to be warned."

"It was years ago!" Charlotte protested. "It only lasted a few weeks."

"That doesn't matter," Ruth told her. "You see, it's not over. It's never over."

"I've forgiven him!"

"You've forgiven him for now," Ruth said, quietly, "but you'll have to keep forgiving him."

She stood up. "I'd better go. Thank you for seeing me."

She would have to call Dylan, tell him that they'd been barking up the wrong tree.

"I'll see you to the door," Charlotte said.

In the porch, as Charlotte was about to let her out, Ruth paused, lost in thought.

"Can I ask you something?" she said to Charlotte.

"I guess," the girl said.

"Did you tell your mother, or did she find out?"

"She saw that something was wrong and asked me what it was. In the end, I told her."

"And she believed you?"

"Of course," Charlotte said, looking confused for a moment. "Didn't yours?"

Ruth hesitated. "Pardon?"

Charlotte stared at her, unflinching. "I could tell yesterday, when we were talking. Your dad did that to you, didn't he?"

Faced with a direct question, Ruth couldn't lie. "Yes," she said. "He did." Not for a few weeks, but for three years.

"What did you do?" Charlotte asked.

"At the time, nothing. He was a drunk. I was scared of him, of everything. He told me they'd take me into care if I told anyone. Later, I rang helplines, got my counselling that way."

"You never told your mother?" Charlotte asked.

"Eventually I did," Ruth told her. "When I was seventeen. She didn't believe me at first."

"At first?"

"After a while, she sort of accepted what he did. Dad didn't deny it. I think he told her it happened a long time ago, when she was ill. But her illness wasn't a real reason. He did it because he had the power to, only stopped when my periods started and it got too risky. I ought to be over it, he told my mum. Only I wasn't."

Sometimes, Ruth suspected that her mum knew all along, just pretended that it wasn't happening. You never really knew whether people were telling you the truth.

"Did you report it to anyone?" Charlotte asked.

"Apart from the phonecalls? No. But I probably should have done. What I did was to move out as soon as I reasonably could. Then I moved away altogether."

"And how do you feel," Charlotte asked, "now that he's dying?"

"I feel numb," Ruth said. Was that the right word? "But I'm going there now. My mum needs me. I've made her feel guilty for long enough."

"Good luck," Charlotte said.

They looked at each other for a moment: victims, survivors, equals.

"Good luck to you, too," Ruth said, wanting to

say more but not knowing how to. She wasn't a friend, or a therapist. She wasn't even a social worker. She was a police officer, bound by duty to betray a confidence.

"Goodbye," she said, then left.

18

Most weekends, Charlene stayed at Ian's house. Going back to her tiny flat round the corner seemed stupid. Today, she'd had him order a full set of Monday morning papers. For once, she was the first to get up, settling down for an hour before breakfast to read what the dailies had to say about her client.

The tabloids went to town on the story. WHAT THEY ALL DESERVE! ranted *The Sun*. HE HAD IT COMING! said *The Star*. TOUGH JUSTICE FOR FREED FREAK said *The Mirror*. KNIFE ATTACK CHILD MOLESTOR "GOT WHAT HE DESERVED" SAYS VICTIM'S FATHER was the rather more sober headline in the broadsheet which Charlene normally read.

All of the papers were careful not to identify the victims whose families they interviewed, but Alan Wallace's photograph was prominently positioned in every single one of them. By being attacked, he'd got far more publicity than if he'd merely been convicted.

Few of the papers explored why the charges against Wallace had been dropped. Charlene herself had given several interviews the day before, pointing out that, in the eyes of the law, Wallace was "not guilty". But her words had been ignored, or, where they were used, twisted to sound like pious whingeing.

"I suppose I'll have to go and see him," Charlene told Ian over breakfast.

"Has he asked for you?"

"No. The hospital say that he's heavily sedated most of the time."

"Then leave it," her lover suggested. "When he recovers he can pursue a Criminal Injuries Compensation claim. But he's not your responsibility."

"I guess not," she said.

"Unless, of course, you've found anything to sue over, or want to negotiate selling his story to the papers…"

Charlene reeled in disgust. "They wouldn't…"

"I'd put money on there being more than one offer waiting when you get to the office."

*　　*　　*

He was right, Charlene found when she got in at nine. The interview requests were carefully worded. One offered to make a substantial donation to "Mister" Wallace's favourite charity. Another promised that appropriate compensation for Wallace's time would be 'discreetly routed' to an account of Charlene's choice. There was also a message from Neil Foster, asking whether he could meet with her. Presumably that was about Wallace too.

The CID man arrived ten minutes after she'd phoned him.

"Thanks for seeing me so quickly," he said. "I won't take much of your time."

Neil needed to know who might have done this to Wallace. Charlene wasn't much help.

"I presume you've checked with the families of his alleged victims," she said. Neil winced at the word 'alleged'. "We have," he said. "Doesn't look promising."

"What about the children he was convicted of abusing when he was a teacher?"

"Doubtful," Neil said. "It was a long time ago. Why would someone from the past suddenly show up?"

"The publicity about his release?"

"A paragraph in *The Evening Post*? That's hardly a lot of publicity. Anyway, his previous convictions were in Derbyshire."

"A vigilante, then?"

Neil nodded. "That seems to be the most likely explanation. We were wondering whether Wallace left any record with you of the threats made against him? Something which might have slipped his mind after the shock of the attack."

"I'll look at my notes," Charlene said, "but I think I told Ben everything that was relevant earlier in the week."

"All Ben told me was the time of Wallace's interview with you."

"There wasn't a lot more *to* tell," Charlene assured him. "Wallace didn't see the people who pushed him into the river. Apart from that, there was some shit shoved through his door, a broken window ... that's all I have in my notes. Sorry."

"Oh, well," Neil said, standing. "Thanks again for fitting me in." He still had some coffee left, Charlene saw. She couldn't resist fishing for facts about her ex.

"Do you and Ben still see a lot of each other?"

"Not as much since I joined CID, but, you know ... some."

"I was surprised he split up with Ruth so quickly."

"Me too," Neil agreed. "But relationships on the job can be awkward."

"Yeah," Charlene said. "So his new girlfriend, I forget her name..."

"Julie," Neil filled in, confirming Charlene's

suspicions that there *was* a new girlfriend.

"She's not in the job?"

"Hardly," Neil said, smirking as though she was taking the micky.

"What's so funny?" Charlene asked, putting on her politely confused voice.

"Oh, nothing," Neil said, standing up. "I mean, she's not old enough, that's all."

"Oh, right," Charlene said, guessing that she'd overstepped the mark.

"How about you?" Neil said. "Are you seeing someone?"

Charlene nodded. "A lawyer."

"Serious?" Neil asked, as if he were a friend, though they were really only acquaintances. But Charlene had opened that door herself.

"Too early to say," she told him.

There was a knock on the door, releasing Charlene from further interrogation. It was Ian.

"There are two hacks in reception," he said, "refusing to leave until you've seen them. They've been told that you've got a full diary all day, so I thought I'd come by and warn you not to go near reception unless you want to talk to them."

"Thanks," Charlene said. "I'll keep out of their way, I think."

"There's a back entrance through the car park, if you want to avoid the 'gentlemen' of the press," Ian told Neil. "I can see you out."

"Appreciate it," Neil told him, then shook Charlene's hand.

"When Wallace leaves hospital," Neil told her, "he'll be a hunted man."

"Even though he's been castrated?"

"Especially after that," Neil said. "Someone ought to make arrangements for him to go abroad, find some kind of sanctuary."

"And you think that's my job?" Charlene asked, incredulously.

"I don't know whose job that is," Neil told her.

"You know what I think," Charlene said, in a quiet voice, "in my gut? I think he deserved what he got."

"I'm not saying I disagree," Neil told her, "but punishment has to end."

"Does it?"

Ian put a calming hand on Charlene's shoulder to stop her saying more.

"We appreciate your input, officer," he said, in his best professional manner. "We'll discuss what you said. But maybe Social Services would be a more appropriate agency to support him."

"They have no statutory duty," Neil said. "Nobody does."

Charlene looked at the fair-haired officer, with his innocent face and earnest expression. He was only a year or so younger than her, but seemed very naïve.

"You care about what happens to him, don't you?" she asked.

"I care about what happens to everybody," Neil said, then followed Ian out to the back entrance.

Curt had been up half the night watching videos, so he went back to sleep after Natalie left for school. He was woken at ten by a crashing in the hallway. He listened carefully. More banging. The sound of a car driving away. A burglary?

Then the radio came on and was rapidly retuned from Radio One to Radio Trent, Maxine's favourite station. She was back. Natalie's mum began to sing along with a golden oldie, Oasis telling her that she was free to be whatever she wanted to be.

All Curt had to do was hide under the bed until Natalie's mum crashed out or went out. It shouldn't take long. Her new boyfriend had taken her to Paris or Amsterdam, somewhere like that, on his Air Miles. The furthest Curt had been in his life was Alton Towers, on a school trip.

He pulled on some jeans, then picked up one of Natalie's pillows, meaning to make himself comfy under the bed. But before he could hide, the bedroom door opened. When Maxine tottered in, Curt could smell the drink on her.

"Nat? I had a brilliant time. The plane was delayed and they kept giving us free vodkas ... Nat?"

She saw Curt, standing bare-chested in front of her.

"Where is she?" More confused than angry.

"School."

"And why aren't you…?"

"Social Services are after me," Curt said. "They want to take me into care."

"Oh, you poor thing."

Curt was used to Maxine's temper, but not her sympathy. She threw her arms around him, enveloping him in a huge hug from which there was no escape.

"Don't worry, Curt," she slurred. "I'll look after you."

She stank of booze, cheap perfume and stale smoke. He waited for her to finish, but she showed no sign of letting go. The prospect of being stuck in a house with Maxine, all day, every day, scared Curt more than the prospect of living on the streets.

"It's all right," he assured her. "I've got a place to go to."

"How'd you sleep?" Julie asked Ben, bringing him a mug of tea at ten in the morning. It was a rest day. He'd had a lie-in while she got up to look after Tammy.

"Grand."

Ben was off work until Wednesday. Today, if the weather was fine, he planned on taking Julie and

Tammy over to Clumber Park on the bus. They could have lunch and a good walk.

"What's it like out?" he asked.

"Unsettled."

She climbed into bed with him. "Tammy's just dropped off again."

"That's convenient," Ben said, the second word almost drowned by a loud gurgle from his tummy.

"You want your breakfast," Julie said.

"I want something else more."

They were just starting to fool around when the doorbell rang.

"Ignore it," Ben said, but then Tammy started to cry.

"This is always happening," Julie complained, getting up and pulling her clothes back on.

Ben went to the window. On the street below, he recognized one of the social workers from the week before. The guy with her was older, well-groomed, senior looking.

"You go to the shop," Ben told Julie, getting a fiver out of his wallet, "buy us some eggs and bacon for breakfast. Let me deal with this lot."

"Are you sure?"

"I'm sure."

"You won't mention him being at Maxine and Natalie's?"

"What do you think I am?" Ben asked, as he began to dress. "On their side?"

Downstairs, he heard Julie open the door, invite them in.

"I'm just on my way out," she said, in her best dealing-with-strangers voice. "My boyfriend will talk to you."

"About Curt…"

"Curt's not here," Ben said, stepping barefoot into the room, which was cold with the front door open. "I don't know where he is at the moment. But come in. Sit down. I'm just having some tea."

They refused a brew, but sat awkwardly on the threadbare sofa. Julie shut the door behind them. She would take her time with the shops, Ben knew, probably go all the way to the supermarket for the stuff rather than spend an extra few pennies at the corner shop.

"You're the boyfriend?" the bloke asked.

"Yes."

"Do you live here?"

Ben nearly answered in the negative. He was still under threat from DI Winter. The Inspector hadn't given him a deadline, but would expect Ben to make a move before he went back to work on Wednesday.

"Come on, Mr Shipman," said the woman social worker. "You were here when I called before, weren't you? So do you live with Julie?"

"Tell me," Ben said, "would it make any difference if I did?"

19

On his second visit to West Bridgford, Neil got lucky.

"Mr Carter?" The man getting out of the Volvo Estate was thirty-four, according to the records, but looked nearer fifty.

"Yes?"

Neil introduced himself.

"I was expecting you," John Carter said. "I read about what happened to Wallace. Can't pretend to be sorry."

"If we could just have a few words inside."

"Sure."

They went into a semi-detached suburban house. It was all pastel-coloured carpets, paintings on the walls and lightly varnished original wood fittings.

Family photos covered one wall of the living room they sat in.

"Your wife and son aren't with you, then?" Neil asked.

"No," Carter said, the lines around his eyes tightening slightly. "They've stayed in Northumberland with my brother and his family."

"Why? If I might ask."

"Publicity. A neighbour rang to tell me that there were press sniffing around yesterday. And your lot, of course. We don't want to put Anthony through any more pressure of any kind."

"Of course," Neil said, as Carter gestured him to sit down.

"Did you tell your son about what happened to Wallace?" he asked.

"Not yet. We kept the papers out of sight. How bad were the injuries?"

"Bad," Neil said. "He was in a lot of pain. And he'll need to pee with a tube for the rest of his life."

John Carter permitted himself half a smile. "I see," was all he said.

"You'll understand, sir, it's only routine but ... I do need to know your whereabouts at the time of the attack."

"Of course," Carter said. "When was it exactly?"

"Around seven on Saturday night."

Carter nodded. "We got to Seahouses about four, had a bit of a kip to recover from the drive, a meal.

Went to the pub for a pint just before last orders."

"Sounds like a fairly thorough alibi to me," Neil said. "But if I could ask a couple more questions. Who was with you?"

"My brother, Peter. His wife. Their baby girl. And we met several of his friends in the pub, of course."

"Did you stop anywhere on the way to Seahouses?"

"Just for petrol." Carter got out his wallet. "If I've still got the receipt, I can tell you where. Yes. Here it is. Just past Scotch Corner. Two-thirty."

Neil glanced at the receipt. It was for cash.

"Something wrong?"

For a moment, there was a wavering note to his voice.

"I'd hold on to that if I were you, sir. Just in case."

"OK." Carter looked impatiently at his watch. It was gone ten. He must be late for work. "Anything else?" he asked.

Neil shook his head. "Is there a work number where I can reach you, if anything comes up?"

"Yes. County Hall. I'm a computer programmer there."

Neil wrote the number down.

"By the way," he said, putting his notebook away, "if you don't mind me asking, why did Anthony change his mind about testifying against Wallace?"

John Carter stared out of the window and took several moments before he replied.

"We wanted Anthony to do it. Think what the bastard could do to other kids if he got away with it. So we put … pressure on Anthony – gently, of course – and the CPS solicitor was very nice with him. We thought he was going to be OK with it.

"Then he started having nightmares about the trial. It kept bringing the … the … original incident back, again and again. With the other family refusing to let their kids go to court, the CPS solicitor said that, at best, there was only a fifty-fifty chance of conviction. We had to brace ourselves for the worst. After we'd heard that … well, I'm sorry, we couldn't put Anthony through it. I know that we left the decision very late, but…"

"I suppose this weekend was planned to get you away from all that," Neil said.

"Yes," Carter told him. "That's right. Especially after the Victims' Support told us that Wallace had been put in a hostel less than two miles away."

"They told you that, did they?"

"They had to warn us, in case we – or, worse, Anthony – should run into him."

"Of course," Neil said, standing. "I'd better go."

He glanced at the photos on the wall. "Nice-looking lad, Anthony."

"Yes."

"Kids are surprisingly resilient," Neil said.

"He'll bounce back from all this." He was trying to be comforting, but thought that he believed it.

"I hope you're right," John Carter said.

"Is this your brother?" Neil asked, pointing at another photo.

"That's right."

"You look very similar to each other."

"Yes," Carter said. "A lot of people say that." He walked Neil out to his car.

"Are you going back to Northumberland?" Neil asked, making conversation.

"I thought I'd do a three-day week, then take some more days' holiday, go for a long weekend. I like it there. I'd move there like a shot, but the area isn't awash with computer jobs."

"How long does the drive take you?" Neil asked. "Three hours?"

For a moment, John Carter's eyes darted shiftily from side to side.

"Only when the road's dead," he replied. "Otherwise more. Took me just over four on Saturday."

"Well, sorry to have bothered you," Neil said.

"No problem."

Neil paused. "That family across the street." He pointed at the window which the boy had watched him from the day before. "What are they called?"

"Jones," Carter said. "Why do you ask?"

"They've got a boy, thirteen or so. What's his name?"

"Todd. But I don't…"

For a moment, John Carter looked perturbed and Neil knew all that he needed to know. "Nothing," he said. "Another case. I hope that you have a good holiday."

"How's your father?" Dylan asked, when Ruth showed up, late, on Monday morning.

"He died last night."

"Oh God, I'm sorry." He came forward as if to hold her, but Ruth backed off, so he settled for squeezing her hand.

"It was peaceful," she said.

"But why are you here, in Nottingham? You're not even meant to be working."

"I had to come back," Ruth explained, "get some stuff. I'm going home again this afternoon, taking the week off."

"Is there anything I can…?"

"Yes," Ruth said. "Two things. I got a phone call from Charlotte Jackson yesterday."

She told Dylan what Charlotte had told her.

"That tallies with what I found out," Chris said. "The house is owned by a licensed therapist. I checked her out. Good reputation."

"Someone needs to talk to the father some time, but with his son missing…"

"If there's no likelihood of a prosecution, it can wait," Dylan said. "I'll get on to the PIU, make sure that the thing's handled sensitively when all the stuff about the missing boy has died down."

"All right," Ruth said. "I'd better get going."

"Hold on," Chris told her.

"What?"

"You said there were two things."

"You're right," Ruth said. "I did." The coward in her wanted to put this off, but it was better to get it over with.

"Saturday night was really nice," she said. "I wanted to thank you."

"I hope we can do it again," Chris said, smiling. Then he realized that this might be inappropriate, so added: "I mean, when you've…"

"It's OK," Ruth said, "really. But, listen … I hope you won't be offended, but … it was also a one-off."

She paused, giving him time to take that in. He said nothing, but looked hurt.

"I like you, Chris," she went on, "but as a mate, not as a boyfriend. I don't want you to think that I was using you. That night, I needed…"

"It's all right," Chris said. Other people were coming into the office and he spoke quickly. "You're right, it was just a bit of fun. No strings. Enough said."

That wasn't quite what Ruth had meant, but it was close enough.

"I have to go," she told him.

"If you need anything, any time…"

"You're a mate," she said, and kissed him on the cheek.

"Are you two an item?" Neil asked Dylan once Ruth was gone. Sheepishly, Chris shook his head. Neil realized what that meant.

"She knocked you back, didn't she? Is that a first, or what?"

"Not quite a first," Chris said, then quickly changed the subject. "Did you hear that her dad died?"

"Ruth's dad?" Neil said. "I didn't know that he was still alive. She never mentions her parents."

"I wouldn't know about that," Chris told him, looking preoccupied. "She didn't seem too cut up. In fact, she came in with a snippet about the Jackson case. Seems the father's got a stinky little secret. You're liaising with the Paedophile Investigation Unit, aren't you?"

He called Greasby over. Once they'd discussed Tony Jackson with the DI, Neil gave a rundown of his interview with John Carter.

"What's your gut feeling?" Greasby asked, when he'd finished.

"I think he did it," Neil said. "Him and an accomplice, who's probably got an equally sound alibi sorted out. Then the family drove to Seahouses in time for John to be seen in the pub. Earlier, the brother bought the petrol which the alibi rests on, not John Carter himself. But even if we got the brother on a petrol station security video, the two of them look so alike that we'd never get it to court. And if it went to court, no jury would convict. They'd be lining up to shake their hands."

"What about the boy?" Greasby asked. "Was it his son?"

"No, our witness says the lad was older. Anyway, the Carters wouldn't put the kid through that. Wallace might recognize him."

Neil chose not to mention Todd Jones, the boy who lived across the road. He had no proof beyond a facial expression. He didn't *want* there to be proof, he realized.

"We need to pull Carter in," Dylan suggested. "Put him under plenty of pressure. There are bound to be some chinks in his story. Push the right buttons and we could get a confession out of him."

Greasby nodded sagely. "I'm sure you're right, Chris, but so is Neil. We have to consider in whose best interests a trial would be. Say we managed to force a confession out of him, which I doubt – you'd make the man a national hero." He thought for a moment. "I'm going to kick this upstairs. No criticism implied. You've both done good work. I'm impressed. Now we'll let the top brass decide on the next move."

Had justice been served? Neil fretted as he drove home. It looked like they were going to let three vigilantes off the hook, completely. The boss was pleased with Neil, but he wasn't so pleased with himself. And Tom Jackson was still missing.

20

Curt waited for the bloke two doors down to let his kitten in, then went up to number nineteen. He rang the doorbell first, gave it a minute before going at the door jamb with a credit card and a screwdriver. He was inside the porch within twenty seconds. The next lock was more tricky, but he couldn't be seen now, so would take his time. The main risk was making a noise which would be heard by a neighbouring house. Still, these places had pretty thick walls. He should be OK.

What would happen if he did get caught? They'd probably put him in Glen Parva until he was eighteen. *The hell with it!* Curt thought, as he tried to prise out the lock and failed. *I don't mind if I do.* Having weakened the door, he decided to kick it in.

He was strong for his size, but it took several goes. On the fifth one, the frame gave. The door landed with a loud thud, and Curt was able to step over it. He was inside.

The Social Services Emergency team leader listened carefully to Ben.

"All right," he said when he'd finished, "you've made your point. I accept that we'd never keep the lad in a children's home and that – probably – the sister is a good influence. If Curt can keep out of trouble, and actually be home when his social worker makes her weekly visit, then he can stay here."

"Excellent," Ben said. "I appreciate this, I do. I know that the home situation isn't ideal, but…"

The team leader shook his head. "That's the official line, but, between you and me, I'm not doing you any favours. We end up putting kids in far worse places. This morning we've got two fourteen-year-old girls in bed and breakfasts. Better that than on the street or with some pimp. It won't be the first time we've had a teenage boy under the care of an under-age, single-parent sister."

He got up to go. At the door, he added: "Doesn't your boss give you flak for your relationship with the sister?"

"I can handle it," Ben said.

He had until Wednesday to come up with an

answer for Inspector Winter. Today, all he had to do was find Curt, tell him the good news.

Remember," the team leader said, "if he's to stay with her long-term, it's crucial that Curt keeps out of trouble and attends school regularly."

"I'll make sure he understands," Ben said.

Now that he was in, a rotten stench surrounded Curt. He swore. The floor was a mess, a jumble of objects thrown randomly around. Someone had already given this place a good going over. They'd finished by doing their business: several times, by the smell of it. He'd heard of burglars who liked to leave their excrement as a calling card though he'd never really understood why they did it. Morons!

Curt backed out into the porch. He'd check that the coast was clear, then get out. There might be some decent stuff left behind, but he hadn't come to rob this place, only to live here. The smell and mess put paid to that idea.

In the porch, he paused. Something wasn't right. How had the burglar got in, for a start? He'd had a look before doing the door: there were no signs of forced entry. And the smell was too overwhelming. Then there was the hi-fi, which he could see from here. And the widescreen TV over there … why hadn't that been stolen?

Curt took a deep breath, then went back in.

*　　*　　*

"Where is he?" Ben asked Julie.

"How should I know?"

"We need to find out before he gets into any more trouble."

Ben explained about Social Services saying that Curt could stay with her.

"That's brilliant!" Julie said. "How did you manage that?"

"It wasn't difficult," Ben said. "There's one thing you should know. I kind of implied that I live here, on and off."

"Well, you do, don't you?"

"I guess," Ben said, ruminatively.

"What's the problem?" Julie asked.

"I might have to change reliefs, transfer to East, or Arnold, maybe. My new boss doesn't like me being with a woman on my beat."

Julie looked dazed.

"You'd do that, for me?"

"Yeah," Ben said, deciding, "course I would. I'll tell the boss when I go back on Wednesday – call his bluff. If he insists, I'll put in for a transfer."

He'd miss Gary, and Jan, and Clare when she returned. But moving would get Ruth out of his hair. And, when all was said and done, it was only a job.

"You're wonderful, Ben Shipman," Julie said. "I love you."

"I love you too," Ben told her, and they embraced.

"Now," Julie said, after they'd pulled apart, "how the hell are we going to find Curt before he gets into any more trouble?"

A table lamp had been left on to make the place look occupied in the evenings, so Curt could see pretty well. There was crap and sick everywhere, but still no obvious signs of a burglary. Curt felt like vomiting himself. He could do with a glass of water, at least. But he was beginning to work out what had happened here. The front door must have been left open for a while. There, on the kitchen floor, was a feeding tray for a cat. That was why. Someone had come in to feed the cat.

A terrible sense of dread gripped Curt. He knew what he was looking for. Tom Jackson must have wandered in, unnoticed, while the door was open. Then he'd been locked inside. For some reason, no one had been back to feed the cat since.

The food bowl had been licked clean. Beside it lay a packet of dry cat food on its side, also empty. The water bowl was also dry. How many days had it been? Curt tried to remember. Five. Nobody could survive five days without water, especially not...

The bathroom. Where was it? No longer scared of being heard, Curt ran from room to room, flicking on lights. The bathroom door was closed. Full of trepidation, Curt opened it. The room was pristine, empty. No one had been in here since the owners left. Curt checked the first bedroom he came to. Another closed door. Inside, it was untouched.

The next door was open. A big room. The master bedroom. Sheets were torn from the bed. It stank to high heaven. Curt found the lights, turned them on. There was nobody in there. He was about to leave the room when he noticed another door, over on the right. En suites they called them – little bathrooms tacked on to the main bedroom. Shaking so much that he thought he might be sick, Curt pushed the door fully open and fumbled for the light switch.

Tom Jackson lay on the floor by the toilet bowl, which he had been drinking from. His clothes were soiled. His skin looked jaundiced. When Curt picked him up, he didn't stir. But he was breathing. Clasping the child close to him, Curt hurried back into the bedroom, picked up the bedside phone, and dialled three nines.

"Ambulance, please. Number nineteen, Riverside Estate, near Trent Bridge."

"Could you explain the nature of—"

"I've found the missing baby, Tom Jackson. He's been trapped in a locked house. He looks poorly, but he's alive. At least I think…"

As Curt spoke, the boy woke. Looking confusedly at Curt, he began to cry, the shrill sound getting louder and louder.

"If he can bawl like that," the voice at the other

end said, "then he's definitely alive. Well done, lad. An ambulance will be with you in five minutes."

Curt lifted the boy up. Tom was very light. He was also very smelly, but Curt didn't mind that. He wiped the boy's mouth with a tissue from his pocket and, for a moment, the baby stopped crying.

Curt carried Tom out of the stinking apartment. His parents should be the first to see him, he decided. They lived a few doors down. Maybe one of them would be at home. He stepped over the door he'd smashed in earlier, then kicked the front door open.

Boy and baby emerged, blinking, into the clear November day. Little Tom looked around, confused but not scared, too tired and weak to cry any more. Curt pulled his jacket around the boy to keep off the cold. Then, carefully carrying his precious load, he walked the fifty yards to number 12A, where he rang the doorbell.

At first, he thought there was nobody home. After a while, though, there were footsteps. The front door opened slowly, on a chain. Curt made out the blue fabric of a dressing gown, then Mrs Jackson's pale face peered through the gap.

"Yes?"

"I found him," Curt told her, lifting the boy a little higher.

When Jenny Jackson saw what Curt was holding, her face drooped in amazement. Her eyes widened, then filled with water as she fumbled the chain, finally opened the door and reached out for her son.

"Tom!" was the word she said, as Curt handed the child to her and tears streamed down her joyful face. "Oh Tom, Tom, Tom."

If you have been the victim of a sexual assault or rape or any other crime, you can ring the following numbers, where someone will be able to help you:

Youth Access:
(0181) 772 9900
Mon–Fri: 9.30am–5.30pm
will put you in touch with free and confidential counselling in your area.

Childline:
0800 1111
– the free national helpline for children or young people in trouble or danger.

The National Society for the Prevention of Cruelty to Children (NSPCC):
(0171) 825 2500

**Look out for the spine-jangling new crime
series from Malcolm Rose:**

LAWLESS: Brett. Detective Inspector
with a lot to prove. Biochemical background. Hot
on analysis but prone to wild theories. *Dangerous.*

TILLEY: Clare. Detective Sergeant
with her feet on the ground. Tough and
intuitive. Completely sane. *She needs to be.*

THE CASE: 1. *The Secrets of the Dead*
Four bodies have been found in the Peak
District. They're rotting fast and vital evidence
needs to be taken from the corpses. You need
a strong stomach to work in Forensics...

THE CASE: 2. *Deep Waters*
Colin Games has died after a bizarre illness.
A post-mortem reveals no obvious cause of death,
but the pathologist isn't happy. Enlarged liver,
anaemia, heart irregularities – it all points to *poison...*

Join **Lawless & Tilley** as they pick over
the clues. But be warned: it's no job
for the fainthearted.

CALLING ALL POINT HORROR FANS!

Welcome to the new wave of fear. If you were
scared before, you'll be *terrified* now...

Transformer
Philip Gross
Look into the eyes of the night...

The Carver
Jenny Jones
The first cut is the deepest...

Blood Sinister
The Vanished
Celia Rees
Come and play, come and *play*...

At Gehenna's Door
Peter Beere
Abandon hope...

House of Bones
Graham Masterton
Home sweet home...

Catchman
Chris Wooding

Look out for:
Darker
Andrew Matthews

Point Horror Unleashed.
It's one step beyond...